The Duke Decides

The Duke Decides

JOHN R. TUNIS

With an Introduction by Bruce Brooks

An Odyssey Classic
Harcourt Brace Jovanovich, Publishers
San Diego   New York   London

HBJ

Text copyright 1939 and renewed 1966 by Lucy R. Tunis
Introduction copyright © 1990 by Harcourt Brace Jovanovich, Inc.

Library of Congress Cataloging-in-Publication Data
Tunis, John Roberts, 1889–1975.
The Duke decides/by John R. Tunis; with an introduction by Bruce Brooks.
p.   cm.
"An Odyssey classic."
Summary: Harvard track team captain Jim Wellington's determination to train
and win helps him get a place on the U.S. Olympic team in the 1936 Olympic
Games in Berlin. Sequel to "Iron Duke."
ISBN 0-15-224308-9 (pbk.)
[1. Track and field—Fiction. 2. Olympics—Fiction.] I. Title.
PZ7.T8236Du   1990
[Fic]—dc20   89-24521

Printed in the United States of America
A B C D E

Introduction

It takes a gutsy writer not to be afraid of small issues.

The Duke Decides, a sequel to *Iron Duke*, brings Jim Wellington, the Harvard miler, through his senior year to the 1936 Olympics in Hitler's Berlin. These were the Olympics that the world now admits should have been boycotted, because in attending them the countries that would soon be fighting the Nazis allowed Hitler to put on an intimidating and stunning show of German nationalist power. The facilities for the Games were masterpieces of technical design, imposing in their grandeur and efficiency. The German crowds were freakishly well ordered. The German athletes were shining representatives of the Teutonic ideal of purity of blood and body—an ideal the world was shortly to regard with horror.

"We were Hitler's dupes," said an American Olympian 40 years later. "He used the Games as an excuse to show the world how much Germany was to be respected and feared. It was Hitler's coming-out party, and we shouldn't have gone." Indeed, the foolishness America soon felt about the '36 Games was a lesson President Jimmy Carter studied—he decided America should boycott the 1980 Moscow Olympics on the heels of the Soviet invasion of Afghanistan.

These are big issues, and an American book that brings its hero to the Berlin Olympics can be expected to address them with passion and high morality—especially a book written in 1939! And John R. Tunis—patriot and moralist—is just the guy to let those Nazis have it in the teeth, isn't he?

Well, actually, no. Because the big issue at the end of the Berlin Olympics in *The Duke Decides* has nothing to do with Hitler and world politics; instead, Duke Wellington frets about being manipulated by the Amateur Athletic Union, which presses him to run an exploitative exhibition race in London, after the Games. *This* is what the Duke must decide: Will he run on command or will he run when *he* wants to? No high-minded moralism about the Nazis; just agony over a personal choice.

We can hardly believe our eyes as we read the last chapter. What was Tunis thinking, anyway? Why, the man shied away from perhaps the biggest issue of our century, to focus on some track star's petty battle of egos with an American sports authority! Was he backing away from a confrontation with Nazism? Was he dodging?

John Tunis never dodged a moral issue in his life, and *The Duke Decides* is no exception. Indeed, by focusing on the immediate dilemma of his protagonist, Tunis has done something more courageous—and ultimately more revealing of morality—than yet another hate-the-Nazis ending could ever have provided.

To Tunis, the "small" decisions about life's imperatives—jobs, affections, loyalties—are nothing less than the truest test of moral functioning. It is how we act when our immediate well-being is affected that shows how we hold ourselves in a system of values; and the freedom to bring our morality to bear on the agenda of daily life is what life in the United States is all about. Obliquely, this freedom is contrasted with the authoritarian reign in Berlin from which Jim has just emerged, where, in a small, chilling scene, he and his friend Helen discover that the German audiences packing every event have been *ordered* to do so. Accordingly, they fill the stands with fearful, bored devotion, in some cases not even understanding the sport being contested in front of them. It is obvious that for a German runner the decision about whether or not to run in a certain race would never be his own.

Tunis saw that nothing is more dangerous than signing over one's freedom of choice to a high-minded institution. And while it sounds ludicrous to equate the AAU, wishing to manipulate its athletes, with the Nazi regime, wishing to conquer the world, the parallel is nevertheless a keen one. Tunis wouldn't flinch from saying that the autocracy that orders spectators into its stands is only a few steps from the one that orders athletes to do its bidding; and that the populace that files willingly into the stands could perhaps one day silently disregard the slaughter of millions of people.

Besides, Jim's decision—and the future that seems to hang on it—*is* important to us, too. We have spent two whole books watching him grow up. His final decision tests his mettle in terms we understand, involving characters we know. To show him merely railing against the Nazis would let him off the hook too easily. Anybody can rail against the Nazis.

It's important to note that Tunis is not making a

plea for selfishness here. He would be shocked by today's worship of the individual unshackled by obligation, when it is roundly stated that "Every man for himself" is the backbone of American achievement, and that by grabbing as much as one can one contributes to society. He was doubtless shocked by the pleas for isolationism in America in the years of this book, when conservative opinion said, "The Nazis' invading Poland and France doesn't concern us! Let's stay home and practice our American Way!" Tunis is saying, rather, that freedom starts at home, within oneself; once you have established and defended your own value, you can extend the defense to others. Instead of "every man for himself," Tunis would probably prefer "you can only give from what you have."

It would be a mistake to believe that because Tunis doesn't use the Berlin setting to vault into a heated denunciation of the Nazi regime, he is failing to protest. There are many ways of protesting, and perhaps Tunis's subtle realism—in which a couple of open-minded Yankee kids intent on sports find their attitudes turning from initial charm to vague discomfort and finally to stern conviction—is the best. It allows us to participate in an awakening, instead of simply demanding that we salute and shout.

A feature of this realism—of avoiding the clichés

that make for propaganda—is the absence of heroics. Jim wins his race, but it is his superb friend, Helen, who begins to understand the Nazis, and who illuminates his own plight in clear terms; it is Jim who shares with us his moral outrage at being manipulated by the sponsors of the London race, but it is Brocklehurst, the wonderfully iconoclastic British runner, who makes the public decision that spares Jim the need to do the same. Indeed, as Jim's resolve waxes and wanes in the last two chapters, we begin to get impatient for him to pull the trigger. Brocklehurst, offstage, solves the problem and leaves Jim sighing with relief. But with this unusual plotting device, Tunis leaves us with something different: a feeling that relief isn't enough, that Jim's personal solution ended one step shy of the finish line—that moral resolve without *action* is, finally, kind of weak. The parallel implications for dealing with the Nazis seem pretty clear. In 1939, this was a major statement, and we should respect it today.

—Bruce Brooks

1

From the platform the Duke looked over that ocean of faces below. Six hundred freshmen sitting cross-legged on the stone floor, trying to act as if they'd been Harvard men since time was. He smiled to himself. Heavens, had he ever been as young as that!

"You men are a highly selected group . . . the opportunity here before you . . ." It was the Dean of Freshmen. That same address to the same uneasy little groups scattered about the hall. In one corner the St. Paul's men, in another the men from Groton, while in between the private school gangs were punctuated by men from public schools like himself. Faces vacuous and bored, faces weak, faces sullen, faces handsome, faces stern, faces eager and attentive. The speaker continued. "You will hear more thoroughly from others about the policies and principles of the University." As he went on the Duke saw himself three years before sitting cross-legged in that vast unfamiliar hall, confused by the crowd and knowing not a person in the room. Suddenly he felt once more that tug at his heart which comes when for the first time you find yourself completely alone a thousand miles from home, alone with six hundred of your fellow men.

And then the riot after the meeting. How it started or what the cause was no one could later recall. They'd all rushed from the Union to the Square, and before you knew it they were a mob; a yelling mob stopping trolleys and buses, holding up traffic, climbing lampposts, until finally they were dispersed by the combined efforts of the Cambridge police and fire departments with hose and gas bombs. Once again he saw the burly Irish cop coming through the crowd, felt that savage blow over his head which dazed him, remembered Mickey catching him and dragging him out of the melee and up to their room in the Yard. He could hear the voice of the man who was to be his roommate talking to the other man who because of that evening was to live with him for three years.

". . . snap to it . . . in ten minutes this place will be full of proctors. If we aren't smart we'll be on probation with the whole class. Put him in on the bed—there, no . . . keep the door open, it'll look better. . . ."

And his bland voice from the next room a few minutes later. "With the amount of work I've got to do, how could I go out this evening? Getting ready for a section meeting in History tomorrow."

"Whose section are you in?"

"Mr. Longstreeth's." And the proctor's steps on the stairs. He could recall the relief even through his aching and throbbing head, and hear again Mickey's voice.

"Come from where . . . where? Waterloo, Iowa . . . and your name's Wellington. Say, that's good! Wellington . . . Waterloo . . . the Iron Duke. . . ." The name had stuck.

Applause brought him back to the big room

in the Union. It was polite applause. The President was now talking. "Take a good look at me because it's probably the only time you'll see me in your college career. Here at Harvard you will find the prime importance of the individual and of independence in thought and action. That is a tradition of the University. There is no mass-man, no herd-principle, for we believe . . ." The words brought back the agonies and trials of his sophomore year when the captain of the track team had been trying to get him to run. Independence in thought and action! There they were in Dunster H 35: Slips Ellis who later was to become so close to him, gray-haired and smiling; Thurber, the captain and intercollegiate shot-putter, a varsity tackle, and President of the Circle; Whitney, the distance man, lean, sinewy, and unloquacious . . . and then his own voice came to him just as it had that sunny spring afternoon, slightly cracked and nervous—

"I just don't know why you fellows came to Harvard . . . why you came, Thurber . . . but I came 'cause my father's a graduate and he pushed me here." That embarrassed laugh from the captain who hadn't expected this. " 'S a funny place, Harvard, but it does do one thing, give you a sense of values. My dad isn't rich, drives a Ford, made all sorts of sacrifices to send me East, so I want to get on the Dean's List and that's why I won't bother with your team. Even if I liked you and your crowd. Which I don't."

Was I ever as young as that? Affected little prig! Back he came with a start to the big room. The six hundred animals stamped their feet and applauded the President. Now the Director of Athletics was rising. "Here at Cambridge we feel . . . every man is someone's boy to us . . . the intramural program which is the basis of the University's athletic program is open . . . a chance for you to learn some game you can play in after life. . . ." Exactly the same talk he'd given three years ago when to the Duke as a freshman, Mr. Horton was a celebrity. To the Duke a senior, captain of the track team and therefore able to penetrate the Holy of Holies, the Director's office, he was only a familiar face like Slips Ellis.

No, not like Slips. No one was like Slips. Slips was the reason the Duke was there on the platform. Slips had come to his room sophomore year after he'd won that crazy bet kicking a soccer ball from Wakefield to Cambridge, and persuaded him to come out and run. Never run a bit before that. Slips had encouraged him, taught him all the running he'd learned, stayed by him when he was on probation, nursed him along junior year into the early meets, the Yale Meet, the Intercollegiates. . . .

". . . and while we want winning teams here, whereas we'd like to have a championship football team, this university does not and will not . . ." The Athletic Director was warming up to his subject in earnest. But the Duke was still thinking of Slips, his friend. Except for Slips he wouldn't be Duke Wellington, intercollegiate two-mile record-holder. Just getting back to Cambridge and Slips again made him warm; it was like Mickey and Fog, his roommates through those two long years, men with whom he'd been through tough times. The open-mouthed freshmen on the floor faded away, and the Duke heard the serious, friendly voice of Slips Ellis in the little room of the Varsity Club, and his own protesting reply.

"Gosh, Slips, a speech! I can't make a speech. Never made a speech in my life. Except for that time at the Chamber of Commerce dinner last summer at home. That was pretty awful. Wouldn't go through it again, believe me."

The track coach, thin, young, gray, smiled across the table. "Now you're beginning to taste the responsibilities of being captain, Duke. Speechmaking goes with the job. Mine, too. You don't enjoy it? Neither do I. Have to do it, that's all. I'm having an argument with Hank Horton today; he thinks I don't get round outside as much as I should."

"Get around outside?" The Duke was puzzled.

The coach started to speak and hesitated. He lit a cigarette. "You know, visit the high schools and prep schools. Some of the other colleges even from the South are coming way up here in New England and grabbing off all the good material. The middle-western coaches, too, they keep right on the job." It was something he evidently didn't enjoy discussing. But the Duke was worried about his speech.

"You must tell me what to say, Slips. I haven't the least idea."

"Yes, you have. You're the track captain. I'm the coach. We both want the same thing—a winning team. All right? There's only a few men graduated last June, but they were key men. We should have more competition and more men out. Last season there were sixty men out for track, year before that fifty, and my first year forty-two. At Michigan where I was assistant under Alec Brown we had two hundred and there's probably four hundred at California. Now look, this is the way I see track." He put out his cigarette and leaned forward. "In a big college varsity football is one tough game. Fact is no one can hope to make the squad unless he's had plenty of training in high school. Guess you know all that, don't you, Duke?"

"Guess I do." There was emphasis in his voice. He remembered that painful attempt freshman year, when as the best end from Stimson High at home, he'd tried for the freshman team and failed even to survive the third cut in the squad. Hadn't even made the squad.

"Right. Now you take track. Take field events. That Finn can train a man who's never seen a discus or a javelin before and make a point winner of him in two years if the man's faithful. He's a wonderful coach. Wonderful, that man is."

"Yeah. . . . I shouldn't say you were so bad yourself, Slips."

" 'Cause I brought you along? Duke, there wasn't much trick to that. A pushover, if a boy'll only come out faithfully and train. There must be dozens and dozens of others in college with ability; men who never ran a bit and yet could make their H if they tried. I heard about you because of the time you kicked the soccer ball from Wakefield to Cambridge. See what I mean? We don't get hold of 'em. We should. You can develop runners in a year or so. You can't develop a blocking back or a first baseman from men who've never played the game before."

"I get you. We want the men to come out."

"Certainly. If we could get 'em out some of 'em will develop. Anyhow they'll furnish competition and help build the team. But first we want to reach them because running is fun, because—let's call it the sport for the forgotten man. The chap who never ran before. The man no one pays attention to in college. I want to see a couple of hundred candidates out this winter whether they've had any experience or not."

"Wish I could say it the way you do. That's what it is, the sport for the forgotten man. Don't I know it?"

"Sure you do. That's why you'll say it—better than I do. Don't worry. Because you're Exhibit A of the man who never ran before he came to college, and a man who made good. Mind you,

Duke, I'm not promising everyone they'll be an intercollegiate champion. You had unusual ability that merely needed bringing out. . . ."

Laughter again. That laughter brought him once more back to the big room, and he blinked as he saw his suave, well-groomed roommate standing poised and at ease beside the little reading desk. Fog, editor-in-chief of the *Lampoon*, was urging them to come out for his periodical, and in between sallies the Duke suddenly realized he was watching the University function from the inside. If no men came out for the *Crime* and *Lampy* they would both inevitably die in one college generation.

". . . a choice," Fog was saying in his smoothest tones, "of making the *Lampoon* and enjoying life, or being condemned for your carelessness to write editorials for the *Crimson*." Even the freshmen, old by only a week, had read the editorials in the *Crimson*. They tittered. And as Fog continued, the Duke speculated on the fate that had given him two roommates so totally dissimilar in tastes and character. Mickey McGuire, Natick High and Andover, completely at home with everyone and all kinds of persons who made up the University, just as composed in a gathering of this kind as he was in the Stadium or the Bowl. A vision of Mickey on the field flashed across his eyes; Mickey, firm, compact, dodging one man, holding the ball out to an opponent in blue and then pulling it away again, deftly sidestepping another tackler until with a beautiful swerve and change of pace he was away in the open field for a score. And there was Fog, a product of Groton and Long Island, standing that cold night before the amplifier they had built in the tower of Lowell and broadcasting the description of the President of the United States at the hundredth anniversary dinner of the Fly Club.

". . . the Dunster Funsters, bringing you this exclusive plate-by-plate broadcast of the Fly Club dinner which the President is attending. . . . I can't tell who's sitting next to him but it looks as if it might be a college man . . . anyhow they've started to eat . . . the President is going after his oyster . . . what technique . . . it's on the end of his fork . . . there it goes . . . down the hatch, Mr. President . . . NO . . . he dropped the darn thing in his lap . . . well, he's trying another. . . ."

Fog and Mickey and himself. The aesthete,

the athlete, and the boy from Waterloo, Iowa. Three of them from different parts of the country and different backgrounds. Incredible he should have two roommates so different from each other and from himself. It was Harvard, that was all. Stuck in the noisiest part of a noisy, drab, and uninteresting industrial city, where traffic makes a deafening din and dust settles over everything, physically perhaps the most unsatisfying university in the United States, but different in its essentials from all others.

Dave Simpson, the track manager, brought him back to earth. Next Slips and then his turn came.

Wait a minute. Slips? Where was he?

Sweat suddenly came out on the Duke's forehead as he looked up and down the line on the platform. He heard nothing, saw none of those faces in front of him, felt only a terrible sensation of uneasiness. Something was wrong. He tried to piece things together. That afternoon. Now what had happened, exactly?

The short, stocky, round-faced Finn had come up to him in the locker room. Kaarlo Tavenen, the coach of the field events, was likable but not very quick or penetrating.

"Yah, hullo, Mr. Wellington."

"Hullo, Kaarl. Where's Slips—on the field?"

"Mr. Wellington, he no come down today. He come tomorrer. He say for me to take charge, yah? Now them cross-country men, you want they should go out?" It hadn't bothered the Duke at the time, there were too many details to arrange and things to settle; but afterwards instead of going to his room he had walked up to Slips' house, a small two-family dwelling between the Square and North Cambridge.

He pressed the bell. Again, and again. Finally there was a click of the door latch. He pushed in and went up the narrow wooden stairs. The door of the apartment above opened and a woman's voice called out:

"Who's there?" The voice was sharp.

"It's me, Mrs. Ellis. Duke Wellington."

"Oh. Good evening. He isn't in, Duke." Her voice was less strained, but her eyes were red. There was something strange in her attitude; she didn't ask him in as she always did.

"Know where he is? Where I can reach him tonight?"

She didn't answer. Instead she looked at him queerly. The Duke felt uncomfortable. Evidently he'd broken into a family quarrel, and his only desire was to get out and away as soon as possible. "When he comes back tell him to call my room please."

"Good night, Duke, I'll tell him."

The door banged. The Duke was glad to be outdoors, glad to be away. And sorry for Slips. Something had happened. Something had happened to that friend who'd stayed beside him those endless hours of slogging on the board track in winter with the icy winds whipping off the Charles and stinging his ears and nose. He could see Slips in his big, shabby fur coat, encouraging him day after day, working patiently with him through the long spring afternoons on the cinder track. They'd been through things together, that man who believed in him. Never could he forget his embrace the afternoon the Duke broke the two-mile record in the Intercollegiates; but Slips was happy that day for the Duke, not for himself.

Now Slips was missing. Something had happened.

A sudden panic seized him. This he couldn't do. This was impossible without Slips. To the open-eyed hundreds on the floor he was a famous man, the captain of the track team, and wouldn't it be swell to be Duke Wellington, they were thinking. Well, it wasn't. It was awful. He wanted to be anywhere in the world but on that platform, especially as Dave was finishing. He sat down to polite applause, and the Director of Athletics rose to introduce the next speaker.

It should have been Slips. Of course. But Slips wasn't there. Where was he? What had happened? It was a tragedy to the Duke as he watched the stocky Finn lumber to the mike in his place. Kaarlo was in agony, his face was beaded with sweat, his hands twitched and closed as he stood there. For the Duke in his unhappy frame of mind these signs of distress were not helpful. Nor was Kaarl's speech, either: it was far too short. Anything to postpone the moment when he must face that crowd alone, without Slips Ellis behind him. Slips, who had always been beside the track in his big moments, wasn't there.

Kaarl finished with a terrific burst of emotion. "You boys come out. You boys work hard. I do rest." And he sat down, vastly relieved, mopping a wet brow with a soggy handkerchief. The Athletic Director, consulting a small memo in his hand, stood once more.

What he was saying the Duke couldn't hear.

Something stopped his ears. But it couldn't keep out the sudden, spontaneous, and enormous roar which filled the room. The Director turned, smiling pleasantly at the Duke.

"and . . . and . . . captain of this year's team . . ." he was shouting into the mike, but no one beyond the first few rows could possibly have heard. "James H. Wellington, Jr., of Waterloo, Iowa."

The Duke stumbled to his feet. Like a race. Now it was up to him.

2

The room rocked, the room roared, the room stood and cheered. "Wellington . . . Wellington . . . Wellington . . ." Then they yelled some more and then they sat down. There was the noise of scraping feet and men coughing. The Duke was on the platform, terribly alone because for the first crisis since freshman year Slips Ellis was not close at hand.

He stood there looking foolish. He felt foolish, he knew he looked foolish, but there was nothing to be done. Before him that ocean of faces, and Mickey and Fog were somewhere behind him making sardonic remarks about their roommate. He waited for the noises to die away. Slowly they died.

"Thanks lots, you men," and his voice was strangely dry, it didn't even carry over the mike on the desk before him. He hesitated in confusion. The moment was exactly like those awful seconds before a race when you waited for the gun. "Thanks lots, if some of you will only show that spirit on Soldier's Field . . . Kaarl told you I think . . . but there's places to be filled this year . . . we lost some good men in last year's senior class . . . Kimball in the hurdles, Atkinson in the jumps . . . they were good men . . . sure point winners in any meet and we'll have to work to develop men to take their places regardless . . ." He paused. It seemed endless, that pause. Now what had he meant to say? Oh, yes. . . .

"The other day a man asked me why I ran. He wanted to know did I really enjoy it. I'd never thought that out before. There are times of course when running is fun and there are plenty of times when it isn't. There's lot of drudgery in it. I suppose my roommate . . ." A ripple of applause swept the room at this reference to McGuire, and the Duke's next words were lost. He stumbled, repeated himself, and went back again. "I suppose my roommate would say football is more drudgery than running, the early season work anyhow. Maybe so. I wouldn't know about that.

"Why do I run anyway? One thing, because I can't play football or baseball or hockey. You can run without any experience. The way to run is to run. Get out and run, that's all. 'Course I don't mean you won't improve or that you don't learn anything as you go along. Sure, there's a technique to winning races. But no one needs to be taught how to run. You can all run. There must be many men here who can run better than anyone on the team if they tried. We need you. Come out. Slips will be glad to see you. Whether or not you've had experience before.

"Now since that man asked why I ran, I've been thinking it over. I decided I ran for several reasons, first because it's the only thing I can do and the only sport for the average man who hasn't lots of athletic ability. The forgotten man in sport, let's call him. But I keep on running for another reason. Because I've learned something from running which has helped me all through college. It's this." He hesitated a minute. Now they were listening.

"You can always do a little more than you think you can.

"Sometimes a runner, and especially a distance runner, feels he just can't go on. But he does. He goes on for one more lap and then one more still, and one more after that—and I suppose that's what wins races.

"You can always do a little bit more than you think you can. That's the lesson you learn from running in races. You fellows here at Cambridge also get something most athletes don't from working under a man like Slips Ellis. Many of you know that I never ran until the end of my sophomore year. You may not know how I happened to go out for track. It was Slips Ellis. He came up to my room and kept at me until I finally gave in and went out for the team. He taught me everything I know today about running. He's a grand person." Now the Duke was in full swing. He had forgotten his earlier embarrassment, he was talking about a pal with whom he had been through some good times and bad. The fact that this man wasn't there made it easier. He loved him and he wanted everyone in the room to love him, too. But even in that mood of enthusiasm he noticed something strange around the hall.

There was a queer feeling in the air. Someone behind him coughed and someone else scraped a chair nervously. It might have been Mr. Horton. Below one or two men in front were whispering. Heads were turning. Then to one side he saw an older man in a chair scribbling away furiously on the back of an envelope. The Duke hesitated, stammered. He was worried. Had he said something wrong?

"So you fellows . . . come out for the team. Come out and run. You'll find out what I found out. That it's a grand sport for the man who isn't a natural athlete, and you'll meet a grand coach. Lots of coaches from here to California can turn out winning teams, but the men on the squad will all tell you the same thing. There's only one Slips Ellis."

No, there was no mistake. The applause showed that. It was spontaneous, sincere. The crowd rose, half a thousand voices filled the room with chatter. But he noticed that Mr. Horton was embarrassed as he patted him on the back, and that two graduates on the platform were looking at him queerly as he went down the steps. Below was a knot of four or five men. The bespectacled gentleman who had been writing on the back of the envelope stepped forward.

"Care to make a statement for the *Herald*, Mr. Wellington? Anything to say about the situation?" The Duke was bewildered. He was even more bewildered when Mr. Horton suddenly stepped in front of him and pushed the man away.

"Not a thing, Jim, not a thing. Nothing to add to what I told you. Our captains are not allowed to comment for the press. Come along, Duke." And grabbing him by the arm he shouldered through the crowd and out to the stairs. They clattered down to the basement and through to his office, the reporters following, asking questions, shouting and calling to the Duke until they reached the room, where the Athletic Director banged the door.

"Sorry, Duke, sorry it had to come out this way. I missed you down on the field this afternoon." The Duke didn't understand. He only knew something had happened, and that the Director of Athletics was upset. Why the reporters should pester the captain of the track team and what sort of a statement they wanted he couldn't imagine. Did it concern Slips?

"You see coaching's a difficult business. The personal element enters into things. Now take Slips Ellis. One of the best coaches in the business. Everyone likes him, just as you said. And I have a special feeling for him because I appointed him. Oh, sure, I got him East from Michigan. I liked him and still do. But you know how it is, the best of friends must part sometimes."

The Duke understood. It *was* Slips. He tried to assure himself it wasn't. "Not Slips? Not Slips, is it, Mr. Horton?"

The Athletic Director looked away quickly. "Why, Duke, I'm sorry. I didn't know you felt so strongly about Slips. He's . . ."

"Gone. Is that right, Mr. Horton?" There was an appeal in his voice which made the Director uneasy. He twisted in his chair. Standing before the desk, the Duke was trying to keep the tears back. After all, you don't cry over things of this sort, do you? Just a track coach. No, not just a track coach. A friend. You cry when a friend goes out of your life. The Director was talking fast, explaining, and even through his dismay the Duke noticed little blobs of perspiration on the forehead of the older man. What he was saying made no sense. Anyway the Duke didn't understand him. The words failed to penetrate the wall of his grief. Slips Ellis had left Cambridge. Slips wasn't going to be there anymore: in the locker room before the races, on the field early and late in the afternoon, walking up to the Square after practice . . . no, Slips was gone.

He groped for the door. "Think . . . think maybe I'd better be going . . . Mr. Horton."

But the Director of Athletics was there first. He reached the door and opened it a crack. "Wait a second, please, Duke," he said. Then he called out "Eddie."

His assistant, Eddie McLean, a six-foot-two giant and a former tackle, came in. As he did so he threw a queer, curious look at the Duke. They all knew of his friendship with Slips Ellis and wondered how he would take it.

". . . and don't let any reporter bother him, Ed, understand?" There was a note of command in Horton's voice.

"Okay, Henry. C'mon, Duke." They stepped together into the crowded hall where bedlam rose at their appearance.

But the big chap was tough. He shoved roughly

through the mob, pushing men away and shouting, "No use, boys, move aside, will yuh?" And he gave one reporter a vicious shove.

"Hey . . . what is this . . . Germany?"

"Aw . . . thinks he's Hitler," said another voice in the rear.

"Who said that?" The big man turned on them. A reporter near him spoke soothingly.

"Thass all right, Ed. He didn't mean anything. Can't the boys have a simple statement from the track captain? If the head coach resigns, that's news, Eddie." But the Assistant Director didn't answer. He shoved along, and then said something over his shoulder as the Duke was hauled and pulled through the door into the cool October night.

Walking down Linden Street the Duke suddenly discovered his handkerchief. Slips was gone. That sensitive man who had encouraged and helped and worked with him, who had lifted him from an obscure and unknown member of the junior class to a celebrity with his pictures in the rotogravure sections, had gone away. They walked rapidly down Linden Street in silence. They only remark was at the entry of Dunster where another bunch of reporters stood waiting.

"Hop up, Duke. Don't pay any attention to the telephone. I'll handle these birds. Now, boys, you know Mr. Horton answers all questions of athletic policy. He'll be glad to see you at the office . . . our captains never . . ." His voice died away as the Duke climbed the two flights to his room.

Mickey and Fog were there and the Irishman was talking on the telephone. "No. He won't. No, he cannot. Nope, he can't. Well . . . he's just come in, but he won't talk. Nope, he cannot. I don't care if you are the *New York Times*, I don't care if it's the White House. No, nothing. I dunno. Don't know anything about the new coach. You'll have to call Mr. Horton. University 5600." He rang off. Then still holding the telephone he called the operator.

"Listen, darling, we have a funeral going on at this number, please don't ring us again tonight. No, not even if it's long distance. University 6453. Thank you." He rang off. "Phew, these newspaper boys are sure persistent. When they want something they go out and get it."

The Duke sank into his chair. "I just don't understand. I don't understand." He didn't. How could, why should they let a man like Slips go?

"Guess there's lots of things about the athletic policy of this great university you don't understand, my lad," said Mickey. He was mad, too.

"But, Mickey, he was such a grand guy. And they never consulted me. After all, I'm the captain of the team. You might have imagined they'd at least say something to the captain."

"Captain!" Mickey snorted. As captain of the football team he knew how much captains counted.

"And he was such a grand guy. Such a grand—"

"Grand guy," echoed Fog. "What's that got to do with it?"

"Well, after all. He turned out a winning team, didn't he? We copped the Intercollegiates and beat Yale last season. What more can you ask of a man?"

"Maybe that was too much." Mickey shook his head wisely.

"What do you mean? I don't understand."

"No one knows . . . exactly . . . there's lots of stories going round. They say Slips wouldn't contact the high schools. Too much material going South and West. That he didn't like being a go-getter, and that Horton insisted he should."

"But . . . I thought Harvard never did that . . . going out and getting athletes. . . ."

Fog turned on him with laughter. "Where have you been all these years?"

"Oh, no, there may be a dozen other reasons," added Mickey, philosophically. "These things happen in every college. Look how they bounced Joe Stevens, the hockey coach. Had three championship teams in a row and then they canned him because we lost to Yale and Dartmouth last winter. And Mason, the Princeton crew coach . . . remember him? It's all strange. You don't know what to think for sure."

Fog thought he knew. "I imagine I understand. This whole thing is too close for you athletes to get the proper slant. Celebrated track coach. Turns out winning teams in his third year. Popular. Everyone likes him. Somebody suggests a man like Ellis would be good in Horton's job. Only a rumor, but it gets around. Bang, off goes his head."

"I don't believe it. It's a lie. He was a track coach and a darn good one. That's all." The Duke didn't believe it, either. But the trouble was he didn't know really what to believe. The next morning the *Crimson* statement was little help.

"Track Coach Edward F. (Slips) Ellis resigned yesterday afternoon. No successor has yet been appointed by Director of Athletics Henry J. Horton, although several men are being considered for the position."

As usual it was Fog who had the last word. He read the statement carefully.

"H'm. Just another case of Harvard indifference," he explained.

3

Any intimate of Slips Ellis would have had some difficulty liking his successor, Dutch Coffman, the new track coach. The Duke found them dissimilar in many ways. Dutch had been trainer and then track coach at Notre Dame, going thence to Southern California, that hotbed of champions. His talent for finding new material, for attracting schoolboy talent and developing it, was unquestionable. Fully a third of the winners on the American Olympic teams in recent years had been Coffman's boys.

Yet his method and his personality belonged to a different school. Slips Ellis was a diffident man; he never called the Duke anything but Wellington until they'd been through a track season together and the Intercollegiates were behind them. On the other hand he was "Duke" to the newcomer from the first afternoon they met in Mr. Horton's office. Slips was quiet, tentative, treating everyone as an individual, never downright, always suggesting. "How d'you feel this afternoon, Duke; okay today, Duke; suppose you take the milers six laps and end with a good, fast quarter, hey, boy?" He suggested; Coffman commanded. He believed in good, hard work and plenty of it. He was an extrovert who enjoyed meeting new people, and liked nothing better than to visit the leading New England preparatory schools where as an executive Vice-President of the American Olympic Committee he was a welcome and popular speaker. And a good one, too. Slips had been a poor speaker.

There was an enormous amount of publicity about the new man in the newspapers—interviews, pictures, discussions of Dutch Coffman, the Coffman methods, stories of his personality, his training habits, his development of Olympic winners, which may or may not have had something to do with the large number of men who reported for track in the early winter. Certainly in numbers the squad was better than it had been for years.

And as a team. Thanks to the veteran men left from the year before, they swept the Quadrangular Meet with Yale, Dartmouth, and Cornell indoors in January. They carried off six places in the B.A.A. Games and broke two meet records soon afterwards. The mile relay team with the Duke running anchor won every race in which it was entered. He ran and ran consistently, but racing indoors was no pleasure. In fact he hated it. Instead of the springy cinder track with the warm sunshine on his bare legs and arms, and that feel in the air which meant spring and gave him a sense of exhilaration and power, there was only punishment of the worst kind. The board track stiffened his ankles and made his legs sore, while the incessant pounding seemed to rock his frame until it ached. The jostling and shoving on the corners, especially the early corners of each race before the field was spread out, demanded strength and weight which he did not have. Consequently he was so tossed and battered at the start that he had to give everything to fight his way up front. Moreover the smoke-filled atmosphere poisoned his lungs and made breathing even more than usually agonizing toward the end. The Duke obeyed orders, but he felt indoor running was a poor imitation of the real thing.

Nor was he particularly pleased when the coach explained he'd been entered in the Studebaker Mile of the Manhattan Athletic Club Meet, the big, final indoor event of the year in New York. "I understand from Dan Horgan, the referee, that Lou Schumacher is entered, and I want to see what you can do against him."

Schumacher! The greatest runner of the country. Olympic 1,500 meter champion and veteran competitor. So he was to meet Schumacher. The Duke's first feeling was one of dismay and an intense nervousness.

"Dutch . . . I . . . don't you think . . . the mile isn't my meat . . . Schumacher . . . that's a tough proposition."

"Now don't worry, boy. Don't let Schumacher bother you. I know the mile isn't your distance just as well as you do. Maybe you'll win, maybe not. I don't care. It's an experience running against a man like that which you should have. I'm thinking of the Olympics for you next year."

The Olympics! The Duke had thought of them,

also, but only as a possibility, for he knew that even intercollegiate stars didn't always qualify for the Olympic team when club and unattached runners from outside were competing for places. There were three places in each event on the Olympic team and probably a dozen top class runners trying for them.

"This race ought to do you a world of good. The first time you'll be up against some real class." Oh, yes, thought the Duke, and what about Harry Painton of Yale who was good enough to break the two-mile record last spring at my shoulders. Class, huh! "Now I want you to get out there in front at the start and stay there, don't let 'em hem you in on the corners, and if you get away there's a fine chance for you to learn something. Believe me I had some job getting the okay to move you down."

This the Duke believed. Everyone knew the Athletic Director didn't look with favor on big commercial indoor meets away from home, and, moreover, as a rule there was no money to send track stars jaunting round the country. They were making an exception for him. This pleased the Duke just as the responsibility bothered him, especially when he saw the news in black and white. The next morning's *Crimson* carried an item about the meet.

"James H. Wellington, Jr., captain and distance star of the track team, will compete in the Studebaker Mile of the Manhattan A.C. Meet in New York on February 16th, in Madison Square Garden. It is expected that Lou Schumacher, 1,500 meter Olympic champion, will also compete in this event. Stanley Davidson will be entered in the shot put."

There it was. The New York and Boston newspapers seized on it, and as the day approached it became plain the Studebaker Mile was the sporting event of the winter. The race attracted interest chiefly because of the contrast between the two protagonists: Young Wellington of Harvard, intercollegiate record-breaker, against Schumacher, veteran Olympic star, a married man and a champion for almost a decade. Different ages, different temperaments, different styles of running. The world of sport was divided into two camps, those who believed the Duke to be the greatest of all distance runners and those who were sure Schumacher would wear him out and run him to the ground as he had every other rival.

The week of the race was also the week of Midyears, not a good time for race training. However, the Duke managed to get his work done and keep some time free in the afternoon for limbering up and practice. The weather turned cold and then warm; it became a wet and soggy week, a period when snow melted and a drizzle fell intermittently, when everyone was sick of work, tired of examinations, of Cambridge, of food in the House, of their roommate's face. The Duke instead of being frightened as he had been, now looked forward to a chance to escape from town.

Wednesday before the race he woke feeling slack. By mid-afternoon his nose was pricking and he thought he felt a cold coming on. False alarm. The coach on being consulted hustled him to the Infirmary, however, where they laughed at both men, sprayed the Duke's throat, and gave him several small envelopes of pills. Practice that afternoon was out, so he went back to his room to study. His eyes began to ache and he finally went to bed. But the next day he was worse, and his throat troubled him all through his last examination in Memorial. Instead of sloshing through the wet to Soldier's Field, he decided to call up the coach on the telephone. However, the coach was waiting in the room with McGuire when the Duke wandered in after lunch.

"Well, boy." His manner was outwardly cheerful, but his anxiety was badly concealed. "How's our invalid?"

"Rotten. Think I'll get to bed and rest this afternoon. If I don't feel better tomorrow guess we better call it all off."

"Now, now, boy. That's no way to talk. You mustn't assume you're going to be sick. You'll be okay tomorrow and you'll win that mile on Saturday. Take things easy and don't worry."

The Duke never felt less like an argument. He ached all over. The only thing he wanted was his bed. Late in the afternoon the team physician visited him, took his temperature, left some more pills, and departed after the manner of physicians, saying nothing. Mickey and Fog came in later with food, but he couldn't eat.

Friday morning he woke up with a full-blooded cold. He was so miserable he was almost happy, for now he knew running was out of the question. At eight-thirty the coach burst cheerily into the room.

"Now then . . . Why, Duke, why aren't you up and dressed?"

"Gosh, coach, I'm lousy. Gotta cold. Guess we'd better call it all off as far as I'm concerned."

The cheery manner of the coach vanished. He became serious. "Can't do that, boy. You're entered. I couldn't scratch you now. Seventeen thousand persons have paid good money to see this race. Mighty sorry if you're under the weather, but we'll have to put on some sort of a show. You see the Club has advertised this race. We can't disappoint them."

The Duke was stunned. He wished Mickey were there. Mickey, he knew, would never have allowed him to go. Why couldn't he scratch? Slips had scratched him in a relay race against Holy Cross when he fell sick with a cold the previous winter. Why was it so important for him to run in New York? But he was too weak to argue, and let himself be helped into his clothes. Then with the coach, his classmate Dave Simpson, the manager of the team, and Stanley Davidson, the shot-putter, they climbed into a taxi for Back Bay. A bed was made up in a compartment and there he stayed, sweating and chilled alternately every half hour throughout the morning.

Leaving New Haven he began to feel a little bit better. The fever and chills abated and he was able to eat some fruit and eggs for lunch. The three men took turns sitting with him, and while the coach and Davidson were in the diner Dave remained in the compartment. As manager of the track team at Lawrenceville and then for three years on the manager's squad at Cambridge, Dave knew the track situation.

"Dave, why do I have to go through with this? Slips scratched me last year in the Holy Cross races, remember?"

"That was another affair. That was strictly a college meet."

"What of it? I'm an amateur. I belong to the Amateur Athletic Association. I've got my registration card and I should think an amateur could run or not as he likes."

"So you can."

"Then why do I?"

"Because, Duke, when you signed your entry blank for the Studebaker Mile you were hooked. You can't stay at home and listen to the race on the air if you happen to feel like it. No, sir. That entry blank is a rigid contractual obligation and don't forget it."

"A what?"

"A contractual obligation."

"Dave, I feel badly enough without your using those big words. What does a rigid contractual obligation mean? If I don't compete they can't put me in jail."

"Can't they? They can do something much worse as far as you're concerned. Ever hear of the A.A.U. suspending athletes? That's what they can do. The point is, Duke, the A.A.U. is presumably composed of you and Stanley and Lou Schumacher and millions of amateur athletes who pay three bucks a year and get a registration card with a number which certifies to their amateur standing and permits them to run in sanctioned meets. But that isn't where the money comes from to send teams abroad. The A.A.U. actually looks out for the member clubs, because the clubs hold the meets and that's where the revenue comes from. Gate money, get it?"

The Duke sneezed violently. He blew his snuffling nose and there was indignation in his snort.

"Slave labor. That's what it is."

"Why, of course. When the club gets your blank and Schumacher's, they're entitled to advertise the fact that you'll both compete. Then

Madison Square Garden is sold out. Now if you suddenly said, 'I've got a cold and won't run,' the customers would feel cheated and ask for their money back. Because the tickets had been sold under false pretenses. So the A.A.U. would simply blacklist you and you couldn't compete in the Olympic tryouts next spring. That Holy Cross meet was a college affair, and the coach can take any man out he likes without raising a stink. See how it works?"

The Duke blew his nose again. So that was the reason for his running. Because he had to. Here was a side of sport he had heard discussed but had never been face to face with himself. It was all true and he realized it. The A.A.U. had him bound by a contract as effective as if he had been a prizefighter.

"Might as well be Joe Louis. Might as well be a prizefighter or a pro ball player in the big leagues."

"Much better. Because any breach of contract by a professional athlete must be aired in public in a court of law. There you have an open court, publicity, and an impartial judge. Whereas an amateur track star like you has his case tried before a board of the A.A.U. which sits in private. And there's no appeal. The athlete hasn't any rights."

"A nice mess."

"That's the reason the boys all get theirs by whatever means they can."

"Get what? How do you mean, Dave?"

The manager started to speak and then stopped. The door opened and the cheery and optimistic coach, made more optimistic by an excellent luncheon at the expense of the Harvard Athletic Association, appeared in the compartment.

4

Decidedly, being the Intercollegiate two-mile champion was not the fun it was usually considered by friends at home.

Helped by Dave Simpson, the coach managed to keep reporters away from the Duke all Saturday. As this was his first visit to the metropolis, New York was curious. Rather the New York sporting press was curious. The telephone rang continually and the doorbell of their suite buzzed and hummed like the Duke's head. Sequestered in his bedroom, he could hear the clink of glasses and the hum of conversation whenever the door opened, but he stayed resting for the event to come.

A long massage late in the afternoon relaxed him and he dozed intermittently, but when he woke he felt almost as badly as ever. His nose was running terribly, and he was sneezing a good deal. To eat was difficult, but obviously essential. He lacked all his prerace nervousness; still, eating was hard and he had to force the food down. Although the meet was due to start at seven-thirty the Studebaker Mile did not come on until ten. To the Duke, accustomed to the variable timetables of college track meets, this exactitude was puzzling.

"Ten! How do they know it will be ten?"

"They know. They have to. Everything's run on a strict schedule in these big meets. You see the radio . . ."

"Broadcasting my race?" That hurt. To run when you felt badly, when you had nothing to offer, that was one thing. But to have your family listening in was something else. Yes, the business of being a champion had many drawbacks.

Well, anything to get it over. With the tables in their suite cleared and the three sitting round—for Stanley Davidson had already gone on for the shot put—the hours dragged. He tried to do crossword puzzles, but his eyes ran so he couldn't see. So he did nothing. Save for that broadcasting he wasn't worried and felt none of his usual strain endured before most big races. It was just something to be done.

The taxi took them through a canyon of lights to a dark street and stopped at a side entrance to the Garden. Their badges admitted them through a back door, and they went around outside the arena to the staircase leading to the dressing rooms below. A great roar came from the track within, followed by clapping and a loudspeaker blaring forth the names of place winners and other remarks. "The bar is at six feet one. . . ." The meet was in full swing.

The dressing room was large but like every dressing room he had seen. The same noises, the same heaps of clothes on chairs, benches, on the floor, the same smell of damp running trunks and perspiring bodies and the unguents from the rubbers' tables all mingled together, the same figures trimly dressed leaving for their event, those same figures returning exhausted to throw themselves down afterwards. The coach found their locker and the Duke began to dress.

Every movement was an effort. Wearily he pulled on his shirt, his shorts, his socks, while Dave carefully tied his shoes and helped him into a sweat suit. The coach was shaking hands and talking to a friend who came up. They were joined by a third man. Fragments of sentences penetrated the Duke's dazed brain.

"Not before a race, Dan . . . hullo, Bill . . . mighty glad to see yuh . . . how 'aya, Joe . . . he hasn't been up to much this week; we hope . . . nope . . . not before the race, Pete. . . ."

Then someone edged round the group and was at the Duke's elbow. He was a short, black-eyed, quick fellow with what was intended to be an ingratiating smile. He had his hand out and the Duke, not knowing what to do, took it. But the little man's words meant nothing.

"What . . . what's that?"

Before the stranger could answer, the coach was at his side, angry and showing it. "I told you this afternoon, Weisberg, there'd be no interviews before the race. Now get out."

The other became surly. "You don't need to be so tough about it, Coffman. I was just shaking hands with your precious boy, that's all." He moved away, muttering something to a couple of runners dressing on the next bench. They laughed. The coach turned to the Duke.

"Better limber up now, boy. We'll be moving up to the track in about ten minutes." The Duke tried to obey, but the mere effort of taking his usual exercises fatigued him. He kept moving, attempting the customary dips and bends, but only succeeded in bringing on an attack of wheezing and snuffling. At last they went upstairs, the coach patting him on the back.

"Just do your best and don't worry. Remember this is only another race; there's nothing in it so don't kill yourself—" The field events were being finished and the track was fairly empty when he stepped out and jogged slowly round the turn. A ripple of applause at the red suit with the black HARVARD on it came from the stands. The noise increased as he moved down the straightaway and took the next bend. He could see people in the boxes looking at him as if he were a strange animal. By the finish line a tall, long-nosed man in a track suit was bending, twisting, kicking his legs into the air. Schumacher.

The Duke eased up and stopped, panting. Schumacher glanced curiously over and came across. They shook hands while half a dozen photographers flashed bulbs in their faces. Over the murmur of the crowd the Duke could hear the glib voice of a radio announcer perched on an elevated chair inside the arena.

". . . and now they're shaking hands . . . the first time they've met, folks, and the first time Duke Wellington has run the Studebaker Mile. . . ."

"Now then, boys." The starter was brisk and businesslike. The Duke watched Schumacher take off his sweat suit. As he himself undid the zipper and stripped down to his track clothes, his fatigue and sickness seemed to disappear. All his desire to win, his competitive spirit, began to assert itself. No longer was he a sick man in a bed in a New York hotel feeling sorry for himself, but a great distance runner ready to face his greatest rival of all. Even in that reeking, smoke-filled atmosphere his stuffed nose seemed to clear, his snuffling and wheezing vanished. The challenge roused him. He jumped up and down. Every atom of his being was concentrated on the job ahead. And as his illness receded, his keenness to run increased. It was a race and he was there to win.

"UPON THE POLE." The loudspeaker bellowed

while the Duke shook hands with the men on each side. One he recognized, George Damon, the sensational new sophomore miler who had, so it was reported, offers from seventeen colleges and finally ended at Pennsylvania. "ON THE POLE," repeated the loudspeaker. "LOU SCHUMACHER OF THE ILLINOIS A.C. OLYMPIC 1,500 METER CHAMPION, LAST SEASON'S WINNER OF THE STUDEBAKER MILE." A great roar swept the arena. Schumacher was a favorite, like all well-known champions. "NEXT, RAY LOCKHART, MICHIGAN, INTERCOLLEGIATE MILE CHAMPION." More applause. "NEXT, DUKE WELLINGTON, HARVARD, HOLDER OF THE WORLD'S TWO-MILE RECORD." While the noise thundered down from above, the Duke stood with his hands on his hips, his aches and pains forgotten; only one thought—the race; only one desire—to beat Schumacher. "NEXT, GEORGE DAMON, UNIVERSITY OF PENNSYLVANIA. AND LAST, ON THE OUTSIDE . . ."

Someone was calling his name from the stands. He looked up into the sea of faces, recognized no one, and smiled.

"Now, boys, no crowding on the turns. The rule against fouling will be strictly enforced. Eight times round. Ready . . . get set. . . ."

Bang.

They were off in a heap. It *was* a heap, too, a heap of mingled legs, arms, and bodies fighting desperately for the first corner where the usual wrestle took place, leaving the Duke battered and beaten in the rear. Schumacher was just ahead, while far in front, as they pounded down the stretch, were the flying feet of Damon.

The Duke pulled himself together, settling into his stride, and fell in behind Schumacher. Never mind those boy wonders, Schumacher was the man to fear, the man to beat; step by step they moved along in unison. Starting the second lap they passed someone. The Duke was unable to see who it was, but by the man's heavy breathing that early in the race he guessed the pace was fast. On the third lap they began to overhaul another figure ahead. Schumacher went past him at the start of the fourth lap, but the Duke had to wait to take a corner and lost ground. On the straightaway his rival was five yards to the good. It took everything he had to catch him.

Dutch was yelling at him as, stride matching stride, they took the fifth and sixth laps together and started for the lone runner up front. Stick to Schumacher. Stick to Schumacher, somehow, anyhow. Above, the vast arena was bedlam. The

Duke lost count of the laps, he simply tried to hold on to those aggravating feet ahead. Was the pace getting faster? Yes, Schumacher was lengthening his stride. They came up to the leader, caught him together. The bell clanged violently. Last lap—last lap. Yes, last lap. Now for one final effort.

Schumacher opened up. The Duke attempted to follow, to step out, to lengthen his stride. Still there was a gap. He fought with everything he had, but the gap increased. He went faster, he pushed himself, but his sprint wasn't there. Nothing was there. He could try, he could dig his nails into his hands, but there was no response. He was falling back, slowly, then faster.

The sound of pounding feet caught him. Was he losing his first race? Impossible. He jerked forward, but the effort almost finished him. On the next to last turn a jostling figure elbowed past him. Head back, the Duke threw himself on. Then down the stretch another figure appeared at his elbow, too. The three fought blindly for the tape together, but five yards from the finish the Duke felt them move ahead. It was a new sensation. The Iron Duke was losing. He staggered across the line and fell into Dave's arms.

He felt violently sick. On the stairs leading down to the dressing room he lost his dinner and lying on a bench he retched and retched until there was nothing more to come. This was different, this was. Funny what a difference losing a race meant. He didn't enjoy running as much as he thought he did.

They carried him onto the rubbing table and how long he remained there he couldn't recall. It was a long, long while, and all the time there were voices outside.

"Well, but, Dutch, you promised—"

"I don't care what I said—"

"Just a few quotes, Dutch—"

"Can't you see the boy's ill—"

"Yah, they're all ill when they lose."

"Who made that crack?"

"Never mind him, Dutch, can't we just talk to the boy for a couple of minutes? While he's dressing?"

"No, you cannot. No one can talk to him. Not now. Come up to Cambridge next week and we'll all have lunch together."

Dave brought his clothes into the rubbing room

and helped him into them. Now that it was over, now that the race excitement had gone, he felt sick and so weak he could hardly walk. Losing races was no fun. He understood why Harry Painton of Yale cried after their battle in the Intercollegiates last year. They went upstairs pursued by half a dozen expostulating reporters. And within an hour of the finish the Duke was tucked into a compartment on the midnight train for Boston.

Sleep was impossible. As the train rolled through the night and the emotion of competition vanished, his cold returned with full force, bringing fever with it. On reaching Back Bay he dressed, shivering, and with the coach and Dave Simpson went out to Cambridge in a taxi. They took him directly to the Stillman Infirmary. At seven o'clock in the morning the nurses were not accustomed to receiving patients, and there was some delay.

However, a bed was finally found, some medicine was poured into him, and at last sleep came. He woke to find Mickey and Fog standing beside him, their arms full of newspapers.

"How do you feel?"

The Duke didn't really know. "All right, I

guess." But his voice was strangely husky, and the passages of his nose stopped completely. For some time nurses hovered round his bed, taking his temperature, giving him pills, and squirting unpleasant solutions in his throat and nose. At last he was able to talk.

"Tell me the worst. What do they say about the race?"

Fog had the sports sheets spread open on the bed. "Well, most of them to begin with mention your cold. One or two are sort of skeptical and one lad says somewhere he supposes stars are always ailing when they're beaten. Kind of him, isn't it? Except Dorgan of the *Times;* he's a friend of Dutch and flatly calls it influenza and says you were courageous to run and not let the crowd in the Garden down. H'm . . ."

"Here's the *Mirror*," read Mickey. "The *Mirror* speaks thusly: 'Duke Wellington, Harvard's handyman, showed up at the Garden last night in what was to be an epoch-making event and turned out to be just another race. Lou Schumacher . . . ran away with the event . . . in the slow time of 4.18.2. . . .' "

"Never mind that. Read me the *Tribune;* Dad always reads the *Tribune* at home."

"The *Trib?* Let's see. 'Schumacher romps away with Studebaker Mile.' Then it says: 'Duke Wellington, Harvard captain and distance star, was no match for Lou Schumacher, veteran Olympic runner, and showed that 1,500 meters is no distance for the collegian.' "

"How do they know it isn't?" snorted the Duke.

"Save your fire, boy. Here's Weisberg of the *News*. It's headed: 'Harvard Boy Goes High Hat,' and explains in detail how you snubbed the reporters of America's greatest newspapers."

"But I didn't snub anyone. Hand me that clean handkerchief. Kuchoo. . . . I never refused to talk. . . ."

" 'Duke Wellington who was once a regular from Waterloo, Iowa, has let the atmosphere of Cambridge get him and gone completely Harvard.' Here's a nasty one. 'He finished last in the Studebaker Mile at the Garden yesterday evening, and his coach, Dutch Coffman of the *Crimson* stated that the runner was suffering from influenza, pneumonia, gastritis, and several other diseases. That's strictly Ming Fooey to us. The point is Wellington flivered badly in his first test against real competition.' "

"Real competition! Say, what do they call Harry

Painton? And Crouse of Cornell? Real competition!"

"I like this. This is good. Hartley in the *Mail*. It's a complete interview."

"But I didn't give any interviews. They can't print that."

"They did. Hmm . . . 'The Duke, tall, lean, tanned, stood beside his locker and explained the system that gave him the Intercollegiate title. . . .' "

"My system!" The Duke sneezed. "Who is that man?"

"Hartley, Rex Hartley, a man with imagination. Like your roommate. I admire him."

"I don't. It's disgraceful. Making me say things I never said. I could sue him."

"Don't advise that, Duke. Besides it's all most harmless and makes you out a literate person. Almost. Your views on running, on life, on holding the Olympics in Berlin . . . on practically everything."

The Duke was in no condition to read because his eyes were running so, and the following morning the newspapers had been thrown out by mistake. Perhaps it was just as well, for there was much in the sportswriters' comments he did not like. Some days later Fog had the last word about the whole affair. He was reading Medieval History when the Duke returned after dinner and a track conference at the Varsity Club the afternoon he was released from the Infirmary.

"Well, well, welcome home. How is our athletic hero? Had enough of running for a while?"

"And then some," replied the Duke with emphasis.

"You should read history and cultivate a dispassionate attitude, my boy. The Crusades and all that sort of thing. Then glance at the glistening row of testimony to your prowess," and he waved at the Duke's silver trophies on the bookcases and the mantelpiece above the fireplace, carefully polished once every three weeks by Mrs. Brooks, the goodie.

"Read history. Formerly we martyred ourselves for an ideal. Now we do it for a challenge cup."

5

Fog was annoyed. That most amiable of all roommates came in plainly upset.

"If it had been the Chemistry . . ." he muttered. "Or even the History, I'd have understood. But English 12!"

The Duke on the window seat, contemplating the frozen skaters on the frozen river, and Mickey, reading the sports section of the *New York Times* in an armchair, looked up. Fog in an irascible mood was a novelty.

"Understood what? What's eating you, Foggie?"

"Got an E. Yep, an E in English 12. Old Jennison's course, too."

J. E. G. Jennison, Jackson Professor of English, was one of the characters of the University. This was a fact upon which he traded. His courses in writing were popular but stiff, and by no means easy to get into for he had no patience with loafers and kept the standards high. Fog, as the editor of the *Lampoon*, felt an obligation to get better marks than the two editors of the *Crimson* who also took the course. That E hurt. Moreover it was the first he had received in college, so his roommates were all attention.

"Thought you did well at Midyears, Fog. Gosh, if you got an E, there's no reason why I should have a C. You did much better than I did."

"I thought so. But you know how funny Jenny is about marks." Professor Jennison's pet hate was the system of marks. "The credit system," he used so say to his class every fall, "is the curse of American education." Marks, he believed, meant nothing; he paid little heed to them and didn't believe in them. Every year his first lecture was spent explaining the futility of marks.

"Of course the old rascal might have given me an E on purpose. His idea of a joke, maybe."

This seemed unlikely. Both Mickey and the Duke laughed it off and advised Fog to call on the Dean.

"I shall," he said with emphasis. "No later than two o'clock this afternoon. I need a good mark in that course; at least I'd counted on it."

The Dean was available and gracious when Fog finally got into his office. "Why, yes, Mr. Smith, I recall noticing that E in Professor Jennison's course and I was astonished. Let me see the day-pages, Miss Smythe."

His secretary brought in the day-pages, small sheets folded in the middle for easy reference. There it was. English 12 . . . . . . E.

"H'm, did you think you did well at Midyears? You did . . . wait a minute . . . Miss Smythe, get me Professor Jennison, please . . . Good afternoon, professor. How are you? Yes, very well, thanks, very well indeed. Professor, I'm inquiring about a Mr. Smith in your course, J. Faugeres Smith. Yes, what was his Midyear mark? Yes . . . oh . . . it was . . . he did . . . h'm . . .

that's regrettable . . . Well, you see through some error it came to us as E. Oh, I'm quite sure it was your secretary's fault, Professor, quite sure . . . yes, it came in an E here in this office. . . . I'm sorry about . . . yes, I know your feeling about marks . . . yes, I know . . . yes, I daresay he will . . . thank you, Professor . . . thank you . . . good-bye." He swung round, his face slightly flushed.

"I fear we owe you an apology, Mr. Smith. The mark was B $-$. Yes, your mark for the term was C $-$ but you got a B $+$ on the examination, making it B $-$ for the whole term. It appears that Professor Jennison's secretary made an error in copying the mark for our records. These mistakes do occur . . . I remember one we had my first year in—as Dean—except that it was the other way about, fortunately for the man in question."

Fog knew Harvard. He understood instantly what the Dean was saying, for Deans talk in a cryptic language as much to be misunderstood as to be understood. "You mean you can't change it?"

"I'm afraid not, Mr. Smith. It's a rule of the University. Once a mark goes on the record at Harvard it is never changed."

There it stood. As Fog said to his roommates that evening, Old Jennison might have induced them to change it, but certainly the Dean never would. And Jennison didn't believe in marks. So Fog was caught.

"Hang it all, with that E I'm perilously near to probation."

"Oh, don't worry, Fog. Jennison will fix it up for you at the Finals. He'll give you a good mark for the whole course in June."

"Maybe. Maybe not. In the meantime I'm on the uneasy side for the rest of the year. What a rule! Imagine, a man gets a B and is given an E because some stupid secretary in copying the marks made a mistake. 'Once a mark goes on the record at Harvard it is never changed.' He imitated the precise manner of the Dean. "Well, I don't care, but it's really Jenny's fault. He could change it if he wanted to make a stink about it. Trouble is his phobia against marks. Say . . . I'm going to have some fun with him. Where are those old notes of my brother Ed's? I've got an idea."

Fog's brother had taken English 12 several years before and bequeathed him a complete set of notes in which Jennison's famous wisecracks predominated. For the course was as much Jennison and the wisecracks as it was anything else. So the Duke, watching Fog read over the notes that evening, looked for some good clean fun in class the next day, and he was not disappointed.

The subject of the afternoon was Jargon. Old Jennison was wound up in his best form, for he hated sloppy writing and loved to attack it whenever possible.

"This afternoon, gentlemen, we shall discuss the subject of Jargon." The class settled comfortably in its seats ready for an hour of Jenny at his best. They anticipated fireworks and he was there to deliver them, although as it turned out the fireworks were to come from an unexpected source.

"Of course, gentlemen," he said, striding up and down the platform, winding and unwinding his long legs as he sat on the front edge of the desk, "of course, we shall endeavor not to confuse Jargon with Journalese. We discussed Journalese at our last two meetings. The two overlap, it's true, but Jargon is used by millions who never wrote for newspapers. The good folk who use Jargon do not say 'adverse weather conditions' when they mean bad weather as do the journalists. They circumlocute, they use twenty words where five would do. They like to vary their qualifying adjective, a frightful trick. From your daily newspaper I read:

" 'The *Crimson* halfback bored through for seven yards . . . the Natick Flash slipped off tackle . . . again the Harvard back tossed a short forward over the line . . . from the twenty yard line the Crimson captain dropped back . . .' Why, why, why, when the writer means Mr. McGuire? Why this attempt at variation which deceives no one and bores us all? Jargon, gentlemen, one might as well be reading a Boston sportswriter." A slight titter ran through the hall. Everyone knew Jennison's feelings about the newspapers, especially the Boston newspapers.

"Let me ask you . . . may I call on one of you to give the class an example of Jargon?"

Fog, his brother's notes half-opened on his lap, made a gesture which caught the professor's eye.

"Yes, Mr. Smith, will you in your great wisdom enlighten us?"

The class tittered once more. The news of Fog's debacle at Midyears had gone round. They waited to see what would happen, and they were sure Fog would have a protest, visible or otherwise, to make. But he said nothing. The professor continued.

"I'm sure you can help us out." This might have been ironical or not; in any event the class turned toward Fog expectantly. They had never found him at a loss for words.

"Do you care to go to a movie tonight? The answer is in the negative."

There was a perceptible pause. Jennison on the platform raised his eyebrows, but immediately collected himself and continued. "Precisely. The example of Jargon could hardly have been more accurate had it come from this fount of knowledge. Do you see, gentlemen, where the Jargon comes in? . . . Exactly . . . in the last sentence. Instead of saying 'no.' Just plain no, n-o, the speaker chooses to say, 'The answer is in the negative.' Another example?" And he waited tentatively.

If the room did not sense the outlines of conflict between the professor and Fog, at least they felt something was in the air and preferred to remain spectators on the sideline. No one spoke, so again Fog made a slight gesture.

"Ah . . . yes, Mr. Smith, you seem to be the

most articulate member of the class today. Another example."

Fog glanced down at the notes before him.

"I was entirely indifferent to the results of the Yale basketball game last night."

This time the pause from the platform was perceptible to the entire class. It was plain that this second remark of Fog's had jarred the professor. But he collected himself.

"Excellent. Really excellent. Again an example of Jargon that couldn't be bettered. And how should the writer have phrased that, Mr. Smith?"

"I don't give a damn who won the Yale basketball game." Snickers from the whole room.

"Exactly. A plain statement unqualified. That would not be Jargon. The first phrasing is Jargon. Now since you are so brilliant this afternoon, Mr. Smith, I feel free to ask you to define a third example. Do you mind?"

Fog was quite ready. "Yes, sir . . . He was transported to his room in a somewhat unsteady and intoxicated condition."

"Marvelous. First rate. Really fine thinking on your part, Mr. Smith. Perhaps you'll give us a restatement of those facts in plain English."

"Why, I suppose it could be stated something like this: He was carried home stinking drunk."

Now the class roared. They began to appreciate the play going on behind the exchanges, that the man on the floor had been using the pet phrases of the professor. And the last sentence brought them down in laughter. On the platform the old man waited until there was quiet.

"Very good indeed, very good. That at least was the way I myself phrased it last year, and if I remember rightly, the year before that. By the way, Mr. Smith, how is your brother Edward? Well, I hope? So . . . ah . . ."

Fog began to feel uneasy. A joke's a joke, but after all, there was Old Jenny on the platform while he was on the floor. For once in his career he wondered whether he hadn't carried a thing too far. Nervously and with haste he shut up his brother's notes and slid them under a black cover which was on the arm of the chair.

"I'm so glad to hear of his continued good health. Your recitation was excellent. In fact, Mr. Smith, as it happens to be a lovely afternoon and I'm anxious to take a brisk walk before tea, and since this course is so familiar to you, I'm going to ask you to come up here and take the rest of the hour off my hands." And he began stuffing his papers and books into the worn old green bag which he invariably carried from building to building across the yard. "Don't hesitate, I'm sure from the answers you've given today that you know the course far better than I do. Come right up. Gentlemen, I leave you in good hands. Mr. Smith will carry on."

He walked down the platform, passing a red-faced and most unhappy Fog who stumbled up to the platform and stood unhappily behind the desk as the door closed and Professor Jennison went out for his walk.

Now, thought the Duke, we'll see. Now we'll see what Fog's got. He was certain Fog could get out of it, but even with his brother's notes in detail before him, he hardly imagined Fog substituting for Old Jenny. An awkward situation. Now we'll see, he thought, as Fog, red and unhappy, stood there slowly getting control of himself. He did not make the mistake of trying to speak over the din of pounding feet which had greeted the last sally of the professor and indeed accompanied him up the platform to the desk. Instead he stood, quiet, more and more composed, looking about the room, until finally there was silence—a complete silence while the entire room waited for his first few words. They came.

"Gentlemen, I'm honored by this chance to address you, but I have an important engagement to play . . . to play a game of Jargon . . . CLASS DISMISSED. . . ."

6

The Duke as captain realized how important the coach was in developing material and shaping the destiny of the team. For that reason he cooperated with Dutch Coffman and even tried hard to put his feelings aside and like the man; not to see in his place beside the track the tall figure of Slips Ellis, hands deep in the pockets of his overcoat and that welcoming smile on his face as the men reported for practice. But things were different, especially to anyone accustomed to Slips and his methods. Slips was always encouraging; especially when a man wasn't doing well. He pointed out your mistakes so you didn't really think of them as mistakes but ways you could improve your form. Several times the Duke had known him to send men on time trials and cut a few seconds off their time. This was done to help those who weren't quite sure of themselves; who had ability but were uncertain about it. Funny thing, stunts like that worked. When Slips told Sam Baker who'd never done under 1.59 for the half that he had come in under 1.57½, Baker promptly went out and did 1.57½ in the next meet. The improvement of one man seemed to drag along in its wake the improvement of others.

Dutch Coffman was different. Not that he was unapproachable; on the contrary he was almost too much the reverse—off the track. In practice he was a kind of lion-trainer, barking commands, urging them to do better, and always and everlastingly telling them to "fight." That was a favorite word of his. One afternoon, before dressing, the Duke went out to find Dave Simpson, the manager, who was talking to one of the football managers near their field. Spring football practice had just started, and the Duke paused to watch proceedings. Beside the tackling dummy suspended from a chain stood the football coach, the man who'd given Harvard three straight victories over Yale, and after all, as any undergraduate would tell you, what did the rest of the season matter? Tim Cousins had come to Cambridge from Ohio State with a reputation for turning out good teams. He was a big, burly, solid man of forty in baseball trousers and a baseball cap pulled down over his eyes, and he stood clapping his hands as each man hit the tackling dummy.

"Nah then, nah then, hard, Joe, hard. Fight, will yuh, fight . . . nah then, Tommy, hard, fight, boy, fight. . . ."

The resemblance in methods between Cousins and Coffman was apparent. If Cousins' methods were successful, wouldn't Coffman's be, also? But what was success, and after all, using tactics of a different sort, hadn't Slips succeeded pretty well? Always Slips, somehow one always came back to Slips. He put Slips Ellis out of his mind and went over to Dave Simpson.

But it was no good trying to fool himself, for the fact was that nearly every week something came up which made him feel further away from the new coach instead of closer to him. The man was a person of another sort than Slips, that's all you could say. When Dutch Coffman asked him to show up at the Varsity Club for lunch that next day with three schoolboy athletes, he felt like refusing. But it was part of his job as captain, so he promised to come round at noon.

The three visitors were all from local high schools, all more than promising track material. One, Murphy, of Malden High, was the interscholastic mile record-holder. Like the others he was unloquacious, diffident, and a large eater. Despite the joviality of the coach—or was it because of his insistent good humor—that luncheon was painful for the Duke.

"We need boys like you, and I can tell you Harvard's a great place. You'll have a good time here, won't they, Duke?"

He started to assent. To disagree meant that he was not cooperating with the coach. But he also felt it necessary to tell those solemn-faced boys some facts. Was he once as young as that? It seemed impossible; he felt like their grandfather. "Good time? Maybe. But this is certainly a place where you have to work." Maybe he was a little hard. But he had just received a notice that day telling him he had been taken off the Dean's List. You couldn't spend your time working as the captain of the track team and neglect your outside reading without suffering. The Dean's List was hard to get on and easy to get off.

"Well, of course, everyone comes here to work." The coach's booming and cheerful voice reestablished the atmosphere of pleasant cordiality which the Duke's words had somewhat blistered. "Like to show you men about this afternoon a little. Got time?"

The three moon-faces around the table nodded assent. But the Duke was not through nor did he intend to be shut off. "Look here. What do you fellows want out of college, anyhow?" There was a half scowl on the usually genial features of Dutch Coffman, and again a frigid atmosphere descended over the table. No one had ever asked that question before. Not liking the trend of the conversation the coach jumped in again.

"It's a fine place, Harvard. You will all like it and you'll all get something here. Now Castellano wants to be an architect. . . ."

The Duke looked at the thick-faced Italian.

"An architect? What made you want . . . what made you choose that? What's your father do?"

"Contractor."

"And you?" He turned to Murphy.

"Aw . . . I dunno. Just wanna go to college. Like to see my clippings?" And he pulled a mass of newspaper cuttings from his inside pocket and handed them across the table to the Duke.

"And mine."

"Mine, too!" The Duke felt like the Secretary of the Committee on Admissions. He also felt disgusted. Apparently these boys traveled round with printed testimonies to their physical prowess. Murphy, who had been discovered by the sportswriters of Boston several years previously, had the largest bundle. The coach interrupted. He started to say something when the boy beside the Duke broke in.

"And I've had offers from Columbia and Penn and Yale and almost every big school in the East," he remarked, somewhat to the Duke's amazement.

"We don't do that at Harvard." The coach was embarrassed. "No athletic scholarships here, no, sir. 'Course, if your College Boards were all right, there might be ways to help out . . . they're a few old track men I'm in touch with prepared to help the right sort of boys to get an education. *Students*, you understand." He added the last three words with some fierceness and looked sternly round the room. To the Duke's surprise one of the boys looked back at him.

"How much?"

The coach was startled and so was the Duke. It had come from the quietest and most inarticulate boy of the three. Suddenly he became voluble.

"I wanna know how much? You folks in the colleges are all alike. You don't do this and you don't do that and then you all do the same thing . . . one way or another. Pete Johanassen, last year's captain at school, got a twelve hundred dollar scholarship from Dartmouth. Like to meet it?"

"No." A voice from the door. It was a strong, firm voice, the voice of a man who meant what he said. The Director of Athletics stood in the doorway. "No, we don't. Is that clear? We don't care to meet that or any other offer. I'm glad this point was brought up right now. Coach, have you explained our . . ."

"Not yet, Mr. Horton."

"Then let me explain our athletic policy here at Cambridge. Only men who have passed their College Boards can become members of the freshman class, and only those who are in good standing at the College Office and not on probation are eligible to compete in athletics. The reason Mr. Wellington did not run his sophomore year, when we all knew he would be a distance star, was because he was on probation. We play here not to win but for the sake of the game. If we can win with the resources at our command, fine; if not, we lose. There is no aid whatsoever given to athletes here at Cambridge, and while we'd all like to see you in the University, we can make no promises of any kind. Is that understood?"

His words fell like heavy smoke over the dining room. Conversation ceased as he finished and the place became quiet. Someone coughed and someone else's chair scraped on the floor. Clippings were folded and put away, and, as the Duke told Mickey later, the boys sat silent and glum. His roommate listened to the elated description of the luncheon, but that Irish face clouded as the story proceeded. His comments were forceful.

"He did . . . he said . . . why, that . . . did he say that . . . what that fellow . . . of all the nerve. . . ."

"Why not? What's the matter, Mickey?"

"That man Horton, talking like a Sunday School teacher. What's the matter with him! Know how he happened to come to Harvard?"

"No . . . I don't. . . ."

"He was slated for Yale. Actually entered at Yale. We paid him more money."

The Duke jumped from his chair. He was indignant. "I don't believe it. They didn't . . . they don't do such things here."

"They do. And they did. It was well known at the time. I heard the yarn often when I was at Andover. He was one of the best ends Andover turned out, and we got him away from Yale after he'd entered and actually taken his room in New Haven. Same as Preece and Middleton and Sweeney, just like Yale got that young—what's his name, that freshman fullback from Choate?"

"You mean Harrigan? That's well known. Of course, Yale . . ."

"See! See how it works? Everyone's ready to believe it of the other man. Of course. But *we* don't do such things. We play fair. You get your degree next June, you're supposed to be educated. Try to act it a little. Don't let your feelings get the best of your intelligence—if any."

For the first time in the four long years they had lived together, the Duke was angry with Mickey. "I don't care. I don't believe it. You're wrong. I don't believe Harvard pays athletes."

Mickey exploded. "Of course not. Who said we did? We've been at it longer than they have. We know how to do things. How do you imagine O'Brien and Hogan and the rest of the boys from my home town got here? We bought 'em. Just like they bought Horton. Just like they would have bought me if my dad hadn't happened to have enough money to send me, and preferred to pay my way. Here at Cambridge we do it in a nice refined manner. A bunch of graduates puts up the cash so the H.A.A. can step out from under if there is any trouble and it gets smoked out. Or a scholarship. Horton came here on a scholarship. It was in memory of Eddie Mather who was killed in the war. Point is that it was given 'for general athletic excellence and qualities of leadership.' Laugh that off. Coffman had those lads to lunch to sell them Harvard. He needs point winners. Duke Wellingtons don't show up in every class."

Still the Duke refused to believe. He didn't

want to believe. It hurt to believe. He couldn't bring himself to believe. Besides, what evidence was there? None at all. To be sure, Mickey usually knew what was going on. Yet the Duke kept saying to himself, "There's no proof of a thing of this kind." Proof of a sort was forthcoming a few weeks later in Dorgan's column in the *Transcript*, "Behind the Eight Ball."

"Joey 'Speed-boy' Murphy, Malden High's four-twenty miler, is slated for Harvard next fall. Jack Castellano, the sprinter from Taunton, is due to study architecture at Dartmouth."

That was certainly no proof, but enough to make him unhappy. All the things he had heard, the jokes, the innuendoes, the half-suppressed remarks in the locker rooms, scenes, incidents which had meant nothing at the time, now took on new meaning. He recalled the stories of Schumacher running in the Coliseum in Los Angeles, taking a plane and going on the track in Newark two days later, how he was paid what is called "expense money," a term with a wide and generous meaning. Dimly he now began to perceive the ramifications of Intercollegiate sport, the mysterious weaving of the athletic octopus through the university and the outside world, clutching in its grasp persons as far apart as Schumacher and Dutch Coffman and Mr. Horton and "Speed-boy" Murphy and Slips and himself. The curtain was rising and he saw the necessity for turning out winning teams, the pressure on athletic directors and coaches to produce victories. Here as elsewhere. That was what hurt. His pride hurt, also—that he had been living in the middle of the thing and seen so little.

The episode gave him less confidence in the new coach, and as spring came it was plain the men on the squad were no longer as interested in track as they had been under Slips Ellis. "We should round up some of these men and see they come out regularly," Dutch said one afternoon. "Get Dave Simpson and we'll drop round this evening and see Barnes and Everard."

"Well, Dutch . . . suppose Dave and I went alone. Maybe we'd manage . . . maybe we could arrange things. . . ."

"All right. Only see those men come out." It was a command. The Duke didn't like the tone. But the coach was right. The two men should come out regularly. Everard was the best high jumper in college and Bobby Barnes was a good hurdler, a sure point winner in any dual meet.

Johnny Everard had been at Groton with Fog, was a close friend, and the Duke knew he'd have help from his roommate. That evening on returning to his room before supper, he found Everard in tennis clothes and a sweater smoking a cigarette with Fog. If he was embarrassed before the track captain he failed to show it.

"Hullo, Johnny."

"Hi, Duke."

"Just the man I want. Why haven't you been out this week?"

"Playing tennis."

"Playing tennis?"

"Sure. More fun, Duke."

"But you won't make the tennis team. And you're our best hurdler and good for a couple of firsts against Yale. Johnny, we need you badly to fill up that hole in the hurdles."

"Can't help it. Too much work in track. Like tennis better. Nice coach, too."

"Now see here, you can't let us down like this. You've got to come out and help. Boy, your points may make all the difference against Yale and Dartmouth."

The other man lit another cigarette. "Don't want to. Enjoy tennis."

"But you must, Johnny. The team needs you. You haven't any right to walk out on us."

"Ha." It was Fog. "The great individualist talking. Look what the captaincy does to a man! Just one year ago, Johnny, he was sitting in that same chair and talking the way you are now to George Thurber and Slips Ellis. 'The Yale meet . . . that's your baby, Thurber . . . Harvard's a place where you do as you please.' Remember, Duke, remember how you gave Thurber and Ellis the gate that day?"

Yes, he remembered. He didn't like to remember but he had to remember. He saw himself now as a stubborn and rather unpleasant young snob. Funny how your viewpoint changed. He'd disliked George Thurber, the track captain the year before. Now he was sorry for him. And slightly sorry for himself. After all, Thurber's team beat Yale and won the Intercollegiates. His team was disintegrating, going to pieces, and the fault was his. As captain he was becoming a failure. There was no answer to Johnny Everard who liked tennis. That was that.

The same evening with Dave Simpson the Duke called on Bobby Barnes, the high jumper, in Kirkland. Bobby greeted them without enthusiasm because he knew well enough why they had come.

"What's up, Bob? You haven't been out to practice this week."

"Dave knows. Turned in my suit."

"What for? What's up, anyhow?"

"That man Dutch Coffman. Don't like him."

Dave spoke up. "He's just a kidder, that's all. . . . Don't pay any attention to him. . . ."

"He wasn't kidding. Told me I was yellow the other day. Don't like it. Or him. . . . Different from Slips Ellis. Work my head off for that man."

"Bobby." The Duke put his hand on the jumper's arm. "We need you badly. I know . . . I feel sometimes the way you do. Slips was a grand guy. It was a bad day for this place when he left. But the team is in trouble, we want you, I want you; please come out tomorrow."

The high jumper was not so difficult. He agreed to come back. Johnny Everard, however, stuck to tennis and the team lost its best hurdler.

The next evening came a letter from home in which the Duke's father described the fate of his friend and neighbor, Marshall Smith, who had been at State. Marshall was a good halfback but didn't like football and decided to stop playing.

Pressure was brought to bear on him to continue, and finally he left college to go to work. "Marshall says for me to tell you," his father's letter read, "that he wishes he'd gone East to Harvard where no one tries to make you come out for teams when you don't want to."

7

The door of the dressing room opened and a gust of cold wind entered with the new-comer. He poured the water off his felt hat and tossed aside his raincoat.

"Still bad, Dave?"

"Terrible. There's a small pond on each stretch and the pits are awful."

"How's the wind now?"

"A gale. Straight up the course. No day for head runners."

Again the door opened and slammed shut. A wet figure in a raincoat and a soggy white felt hat with blue numerals on it came in. "First call for the mile. Last call for the high hurdles." As he went out the three hurdlers rose stiffly, threw off their blankets, and began exercising to start their circulation. The Duke went across the room where the trainer was taping a tender ankle. "Don't let 'em jump you, Bill. Stay with 'em every minute. You can do it, you got the stuff there. . . ."

"Hell I can. Not this weather."

"Forget it, boy. You showed us all in your time trials. . . ."

"Yeah, not this weather though."

"Never mind the rain. Go out and run. It's just as hard for them as for us." He slapped him on the shoulder and went over to young Crane, a sophomore find who had only been running a few months. The boy was lying in his track suit on a bench and his face was gray. The Duke knew what he was going through.

"How you feel, Tommy?"

"Rotten." He tried a smile, but it didn't come off. The Duke recalled his first race, his nausea and agony while waiting for the starter's gun, and he remembered how Slips Ellis had encouraged him and helped him through these moments. He leaned over and pulled a blanket across the figure on the bench.

"Thanks."

"Better?"

"Yeah . . . but jess the same I feel bad. Sick." The Duke looked at him closely and anxiously. The boy's points were needed in the mile.

"Here. Take a wad of this gum. Chew. Chew hard. That'll make you feel better. Never mind your nerves. If you're sick, that's fine. Sure it is. Means you'll run well. I was like that always before my big races last year. That's right, chew hard."

Dutch Coffman came across, anything but his usual jovial self. He was worried and curt, and there were lines in his forehead.

"Take it easy, Duke. Get off your feet awhile. Remember, you've got two events this afternoon. . . ."

The Duke tried to rest but couldn't. He slapped the hurdlers on the back as they went out into the deluge, and shook hands with Phil Evans, the pole vaulter, who like everyone else was growling about the weather.

"Just as hard for Jack Davis as it is for you, Phil." Davis was the Yale captain, and he and Evans had been rivals all through college. "Go out and show that bluebird up; your last chance, kid."

A wet head was stuck through the door. "Last call for the jumpers. Second call for the mile. First call for the quarter."

Dave burst in and slammed the door. Streams of water ran off his coat and hat, but his tone was jubilant. "Henry won the hundred. Spike pulled out a third." A slight yell lifted some of the grimness from the dressing room. The hundred had been given to Yale in advance.

"All right, you men, if Henry can come through like that in the rain, there's no reason the rest of the team can't. Let's go, Harvard. I want all the distance men over here in this corner for a minute before we go out." Half a dozen hooded and muffled figures rose at the Duke's command and joined him in a corner of the room.

Unfortunately it was Harvard's turn to run at Yale. There was a deluge in New Haven, but in Cambridge the sun shone all day. A ball game took place under blue skies on Soldier's Field, and Mickey returned to his room afterwards wondering how the Duke had made out. He turned the radio on, hoping for news. There were accounts of the Red Sox in New York, the Bees in Chicago, and the running of the Preakness in Maryland. Hardly any time was left when the speaker gave him the news he wanted.

"The Harvard crew won the triangular races on the Severn this afternoon in a gale of wind; time, ten minutes, sixteen and three tenths seconds. Navy second and Columbia third. Down at New Haven the Yale track team swamped the Crimson in a torrent of rain, score—Yale 84½, Harvard 50½; one of the worst beatings administered in the history of the sport."

Fog got the news walking down to his room after dinner. He bought a late edition of the *Traveller* and discovered the story on the sports page. "YALE SWAMPS HARVARD IN RAIN. The Yale track team handed Harvard the worst licking in years in a downpour on Yale Field this afternoon, winning by the one-sided score of 84½ to 50½. Henry Davenport, Harvard's sophomore, surprised everyone by taking the hundred and the two-twenty, and Duke Wellington, the Crimson Captain, won the mile and two mile in slow times, but except for these events Harvard did not win a first all afternoon."

Meanwhile back in New Haven the squad had bathed, dressed, and was en route for home. The football squad traveled in special cars of their own, but the track team merely went in ordinary Pullmans. For this the Duke was glad. Traveling with a beaten team is not much fun, and when it's segregated in a car alone the gloom is thicker still. He was content to have strangers round because it meant less chance for everyone to post-mortem, fewer opportunities for the use of that word "if." How one got to dislike that word. Made him almost hate his teammates, for he had been hearing it continually since the end of the meet. *If* they'd been meeting Yale on Soldier's Field . . . *if* there had been decent weather . . . *if* Johnny Everard hadn't considered himself a tennis player . . . *if* the field judges hadn't been prejudiced. . . . What was the use? 84½ to 50½. That was the only thing that counted. "They pay off on results in this life," Slips used to tell them.

84½ to 50½. Worst defeat in Harvard's track history. Yes, and as captain he was responsible. You might if and but, you might hedge and crawl, but the captain led the team and if they won he got the credit. With sickening clearness he recalled coming back to college that fall, hopeful of repeating George Thurber's victory in the Intercollegiates of the previous year. And now—his team couldn't even beat Yale. Not an extraordinary Yale team, either.

Any way you looked at it, he was a failure. No one said so, on the contrary they were all kind and generous, even the disappointed and weary coach. Most of the team came up diffidently, trying to apologize for their own bad showing or to console him for the licking by mentioning his wind- and rain-swept victories in the distance runs.

"Nice work, Duke." "Great race you ran, Duke." "Duke, you're some mudder all right." "Fine stuff, Duke, pulling out those two firsts." But he knew the truth. He had run mediocre races. There was no one to beat, for Harry Painton had graduated. And he wasn't thinking about himself, he was feeling for the team. In the diner he sat down alone at an empty table and nobody sat beside him, for while they were all sorry for him they were embarrassed about the size of the defeat and anything but anxious to talk to their captain. Only Tom Crane paused as he came down the aisle.

"Mind if I sit down, Cap?"

"No, Tom, of course, sit down."

"Thanks. I'm hungry. And tired, too. . . ." The Duke looked at him enviously. He himself couldn't eat; the bitterness and disappointment of the afternoon had taken away his appetite, but this youngster was keen and hungry.

"And I only ran one race. You must be dead, you ran 'em both. Takes lots out of you—running."

"It's not the running." The Duke thought back bitterly to his victories in the previous spring. He saw himself coming into the dining room of Dunster with Mickey proudly striding beside him, heard the tinkle of glassware as the crowd perceived him, saw again the familiar patch of sunlight on the floor near his table, and for half a second felt that surge of emotion of the happy day a year ago. He remembered his freshness and how lighthearted he'd been after dinner when they went in town to a show. "Nope. It's not the running, Tom, that tires you out, it's the losing."

"You mean losing the meet? Is that it? Makes you more tired, does it? Why?"

"Dunno." The Duke tried to chew on some stringy dining-car roast beef. Impossible to eat. "Can't say. That's how it is. When you win, you feel fine. When you lose, it's hell. Just plain hell. Takes it out of you to lose."

The strange fact was the Duke had never analyzed his feelings after a race, but it was so. Losing took it out of you. One reason he'd never thought about it much was because he'd never lost. Save for that fiasco in the Studebaker Mile, which was no true test, he'd never lost a race and, more important, never run on a losing team. A new experience. Not a pleasant one, either. He tried to be philosophical. Well, someone had to lose. It didn't come off.

"I wish, Duke, I wish, you know, I could tell you . . . Thank you for hauling me through that mile, today. Gosh, I'm proud."

The boy's face was beaming. Made the Duke feel like his grandfather. "No, Tom, you ran a good race. Difficult conditions, too. I was proud of you."

"Were you? Really?" He looked up quickly. "Just the same, I was licked, I mean on the third lap. If you hadn't fallen back and encouraged me, I know I couldn't have stayed the pace. Don't know how you dared take chances. . . ."

The Duke smiled for the first time that afternoon. "I knew I could win. No good distance

men on their team since Harry Painton graduated. Boy, there was a runner, and a game fighter,
too." His mind went back to his races against
Painton in the sunny days of the spring before.
A happy time. Happy because, he reflected, he
was winning and on a winning team. This was
different.

"Yes, but, Duke, it was wonderful all the
same, your staying with me like that, and then
coming back and hauling me up along; it was
sort of . . . it was teamwork like you always talk
about. Now I understand. Lots of things you
don't realize until you live them. I never imagined how much difference it meant when a man's
out there alone to have someone you know come
along and help. George Palmer said you did the
same thing when he fell behind in the two mile."

The boy was devouring his meat while he
talked. In between mouthfuls he went on. "Know
what I think . . . Duke . . . know what I
think . . . think you're one great captain, Duke,
a grand captain. . . ."

Funny? It would have been, but not that evening. For the Duke was exhausted, licked in
body and spirit. And that affectionate boy was
only rubbing it in. He gulped his milk and rose.

"Thanks lots, Tommy. You'll do the same thing next year. On a better team, I hope." So down the aisle, men staring at him curiously from under their lowered gaze as he left the diner and went into the Pullman. It was New London, and a few minutes later a newsboy came through the car. "Evening editions. Five star final. New Haven *Register* with complete account of the track meet. Yale wins by large score. . . ."

Slowly the car filled. The men returned, warmed and cheered by food. They broke up into groups, playing cards and talking. Snatches of conversation came down the aisle, the usual locker-room stuff that everyone said after every lost race, that half-resigned, half-angry tone instead of the jubilant expressions of delight to which the Duke was accustomed. "Thought I had him on the last lap, the rat came up fast on the curve and cut in . . . bar at five eleven and a half, and my foot just caught the edge on the last try. . . . Yeah, thass all right, but what can you expect in weather like that. . . . I told him our pits at Cambridge were never like that . . . gave me the elbow in the ribs . . . right here . . . like that . . . on the last turn. . . ."

Excuses. Then more excuses. Funny how defeat reacted on different characters. Some of them were curled in their seats like sore bears. Others were explaining why they lost, how they lost, what made them lose when they should have won, would have won in normal conditions. A few were reading *Life* or the *Reader's Digest*, one or two had managed to forget the dismal afternoon and were working. But excuses still rang up and down the car. This made him feel worse. What was the good of talking about it; they were beaten and beaten badly and that was that.

Back Bay was ages away. At last they piled out and into the waiting buses. A difference, the Duke reflected, from their exuberant entraining, the horseplay and yelling as they boarded the New Haven train. Now they were returning licked, hopelessly outclassed, and he was captain of the team.

Back home in Waterloo, his father was putting on his reading glasses in his chair under the lamp and looking over the front page of the *Evening Courier*. "Wait a minute . . . no . . . don't think it's here . . . Michigan-Iowa . . . Kansas-Kansas Aggie . . . Ohio State-Northwestern . . . hold on . . . Chicago-Drake . . . no . . . yes, here 'tis, Mother . . whew . . . well, Yale 84½, Harvard 50½. What on earth do you suppose happened? What could have happened to the boy? To them? I b'lieve I'll call him up and find out. Guess I'll spend the two sixty and just see if he's all right. What say, Mother?"

"Oh, do. Do, Jim. Call him up, I hope he isn't sick or something. Maybe he couldn't run. That's probably it, he must have a cold and couldn't run, don't you suppose?" And as Mr. Wellington put in the call she picked up the *Courier* to make sure for herself. There it was, Yale 84½, Harvard 50½. Well, that settled things, Jim just couldn't have run. She knew he hadn't run because Harvard had never been beaten since he'd started racing. Maybe something was the matter with him. She hoped not and yet she half hoped there was, for she felt it wasn't good for the boy. Already someone downtown had mentioned him as a possibility for the coming Olympic team, and she saw herself going through another period of anxiety. Secretly she wished he wouldn't make the Olympic team, for she felt it was too much, no matter what her husband said. The telephone rang.

She noticed his hand tremble as he picked it up.

"That you, Jim? That you, boy . . . yes, dad, . . . how are you? You are? Oh, nothing, just thought I'd call up and find out what happened . . . yep, I know Yale won . . . oh, I see, you did . . . that's fine. . . ." There was a long silence. The expression on her husband's face changed. "I'd say so . . . I'd say that was the way to take it . . . no one can do any more . . . mighty glad you take it that way . . . how was your time . . . slow . . . in the mile . . . you ran the two-mile, too . . . yes, I suppose so . . . yes, I know you don't feel so good tonight. Don't let 'em get you down, Jim. That's right. She's first rate. Sends her love . . . Want to talk to her? Here, Mother."

"Hullo, Mother."

"You all right, Jim?" She wanted reassurance.

"All right but tired, Mother. Be okay tomorrow."

"Do take care of yourself, Jim. Harry Davis had to come home from Drake, a nervous breakdown. . . . I hope you aren't doing too much. . . ."

"Now, Mother." He was impatient. Her husband was talking. "Wait a minute, Jim . . . what's that . . . oh, your father says to tell you better luck next time. . . ."

"All right, Mother." His voice sounded throaty. "Good-bye, Mother dear."

"Good-bye, Jim." And she rang off.

His father was wiping his forehead, and then he filled his pipe. "Well, well, that *was* a surprise. Poured all day in New Haven, Mother, I expect that made a big difference, he won't say so, though. Says they were beaten by a better team, that's all. I like for him to take it that way. Got to learn to take his defeats, same as the rest of us. But it's hard, must be a disappointment, after all the meets they won last year. Then his being captain, it's pretty tough to lose like that when he's captain. Oh, yes, he's all right. Guess he isn't very happy tonight, though."

He wasn't. He was far off and alone, and while it helped to talk to his family and made him warm and glowing for a few seconds, it hurt, too. The moment he rang off he felt more alone than ever. There was the desperate feeling of failure which had haunted him through his first two years, those years when he'd tried to make the freshman football team in vain, when he'd gone almost friendless save for Mickey and Fog, when he'd narrowly missed being thrown out of college, when he'd spent his time working to get off probation, in short when he was a failure, a complete failure, letting down his father who had counted on his doing well. This was worse. Then he was unknown, only another member of the freshman class. Now he was known, he was the Intercollegiate two-mile champion, captain of the track team. And a failure.

He went into the bedroom and lay down. Below in the court someone was shouting.

"Oh, Rhinehart . . . Rhinehart. . . ."

He was in Cambridge. Suddenly he became homesick, acutely homesick for Waterloo and the plains, and the Iowa mud and the house, and the family and Spot, the Airedale, always a consoler in any hour of trouble. Spot would come upstairs and push open the door of his room, and shove a cold muzzle into his hand, and lie on the floor beside him, tail gently thumping. He could hear it, that tail, thump-thump, thump-thump. The Iron Duke, national two-mile record-holder, suddenly gave way. He was unable to hold in any more. Tears came and he cried.

8

The day of reckoning had arrived.

It was May, the reading period, during which no classes were held. Now all social activities had ceased, all team schedules were held up or suspended, lights were burning in every room in every house or dormitory at night, extra chairs were necessary in the reading room in the Widener Library, and college was getting ready as best it could for the last great test of all: final examinations.

Soon the undergraduate world, or portions of it, would pour every morning into the fastnesses of Memorial Hall where rows and rows of bent backs would lean over little blue books, while owl-faced proctors circulated back and forth, pausing occasionally to whisper to each other or write the time in big letters on a blackboard. Then the taut, dry voice. "Gentlemen, in twenty minutes the examination will be over," followed by sounds and clatter of men rising, pushing back their chairs, walking up to hand in their books and going out with relief into the warm sunlight to greet each other with questions.

"How'd you hit it, Bill? What about you, Jake?" "Me, oh, I creamed it." "Not me, it knocked me for a loop." "Gee, I'm bushed, let's go to a movie tonight." "What'd you do with that spot question on Henry VIII and the Church?" "You did . . . it is . . . swell, then I cracked that one."

The days of reckoning had arrived, the saddest, maddest days of the year when spring called but work beckoned even more insistently to the members of the senior class. Nearing the end of their common life, the Dunster Funsters took things each in his own way. Mickey worked furiously night after night to make up lost time. Fog went to a tutoring school in the Square for three hours every day and was still able to joke. " 'How does spring affect your attitude toward Harvard?' the *Crimson* reporter asked the Radcliffe girl. 'Nothing could,' was the curt reply. Ah, me. . . ." And sitting on the window seat while four crews paddled down the river followed by the coaching launch like a hen chasing her chicks, the Duke in a more serious mood turned his father's note in his hand and read it again.

"DEAR JIM:

"We were all pleased in Waterloo to learn you won your race in the Intercollegiates. Your letter here today sounds discouraged, but you must bear in mind that you aren't responsible for the failure of the team to make a better showing. I think it's fine that by winning that two miles in the Intercollegiates you get a chance to make the Olympic team going to Germany, and if you do I'll let you have some money to travel the rest of the summer in Europe. It would be a grand chance for you. Your mother says she'll be glad when your running days are over; but you know what she is. Our plans are not certain, but if business holds up we may drive East for your Commencement, spend a few days with you, and go on to New York to watch you run in the Olympic tryouts at Randalls Island. It seems hardly possible we've never yet seen you run. . . ."

But he didn't want his family East. That would spoil things, that was just what he didn't want. Fathers were like that, always showing up at the wrong time. He definitely hoped the family wouldn't come East for Commencement; for in the first place he wasn't sure there'd be any Commencement for him. As yet he hadn't passed his Divisionals and anything could happen. There was another reason. The nominations of class officers had appeared several days previously in the *Crimson* and his name was not on the list for a single office. This was a big disappointment because, as a rule, the three marshals were chosen from the captains of the major teams. So he hoped to get his degree with as little fuss as possible and move on to New York alone, and he decided to write home suggesting that it would hardly be worthwhile for the family to come East for such a short while.

That evening after dinner when the Duke had

gone to the Library to work, Mickey and Fog discussed things. As captain of the winning football team against Yale, Mickey was certain to be chosen First Marshal, while Fog was sure to be picked for Ivy Orator by a large margin. There was only one Mickey in the class and only one Fog, too. But both felt the injustice that had been done their roommate.

"It isn't as if he was captain of the track team only. Lots of track captains don't get a class office. But he's the Intercollegiate two-mile record-holder and most likely to be a member of the Olympic team, he's made a name for himself outside college. What's it matter if his team did badly? That's not his fault, he won all his races. I think their leaving him off was a shabby trick. At least they might have picked him for some minor office."

"Yes, but you miss the point, Mickey." Unlike the warm-hearted Irishman, Fog approached the problem without sentiment. "He's not in with the Circle crowd. You know it, I know it, so does he. Everyone realizes how he's fought them. Remember last year when they promised to take him in if he'd run in the Intercollegiates and save George Thurber's team, and how when it was over he turned them down flat. That burned 'em up. Naturally enough, those babies never forget. Then he beat their candidate for captain of the team last year, and again last week he licked 'em by putting Tom Stickney across for next year's captain. You have to be practical about these problems. The Circle crowd controls the nominating committee and it seems to me you can hardly blame them for leaving off a man who won't play ball with 'em."

"Look, here's what I blame 'em for. I blame 'em for leaving a representative member of the class off the list. Look at some of the birds they picked, a lot of dopes. Even Spencer Morgan, what is he but just another varsity tackle—"

"Ah, you forget. Point is, Spencer Morgan is president of the Circle. My boy, the Circle controls the committee, the Circle is the committee, let's say. Besides, Mickey, what does it matter whether the Duke wears a red tassel on his cap and red pipings on his gown at Commencement? He's done a swell job starting from scratch. Why not let it go at that?"

"You can afford to be philosophical because you're in the Circle and you'll be Ivy Orator; nobody else wants the job or could do it. But it's tough on him. He feels it on account of his dad. I believe his father wants to come East for Commencement and because he isn't a class officer the Duke feels badly and is trying to shove him off. You know. Captain of a losing team, no class office, while you're Ivy Orator and I'm one of the marshals. . . ."

"First Marshal, Mickey."

"Well, anyhow, a marshal. To have him left completely out of things like that, not even on the Class Day Committee, that's a tough one. Wish there was something we could do, there ought to be some way to put the Dunster Funsters across together for the last time. If you hadn't slipped, Fog . . ."

Mickey kept after Fog for the next few days about it, taunting him with lack of imagination and suggesting that the Dunster Funsters, who had gone through thick times and thin for the best part of three years, ought not to leave college with one member of the gang unhappy and discouraged. He challenged Fog's resourcefulness to find some solution. At first Fog paid no attention, but some investigation showed that other members of the class felt the same way about the situation, and one of them, Derry Talbot, the half miler on the track team and a friend of the Duke's, came up to their room to blow off steam.

"Why, it's an outrage, Fog. When you consider how hard he worked all year. Don't forget, the captain of a losing team works just as hard and takes as much punishment as the captain of a winning one."

"I know, more maybe," said Mickey.

"Well, boys, I've been thinking things over for a couple of days, and there ought to be some way we could work the matter out. Maybe now . . ."

"What? How?" asked the other two together. They knew Fog could do it if anyone could.

"Well, maybe, just maybe, you understand, there's a way out. I've been looking up the rules about the nominations of class officers."

"Oh." There was disappointment in their tone. "We did that. The nominations are closed."

"Yes, but I went back and looked it all up. Dug out the original rules for nominations in the *Crimson* office which tells the whole story. The nominations are closed, but there's one way we might work it if we were fast enough."

"What's that?"

"Nomination by petition."

The others looked up. Nomination by petition! "What's that mean?"

"It means you petition after the nominations are closed to put a name on the ballot. You must have a hundred members of the class sign the petition and it must be presented four days before election. Then his name goes on the ballot."

"Holy catfish. Four days. That's pretty tight shooting. Less see, election's Friday, that means . . . that means . . . Monday night. Only three days to work in, and over a weekend when half the college is away."

"Not just before exams, they aren't. Anyhow, that's all the time we've got. What say, you men?"

"I say, let's go."

"So do I. And not a word to the Duke."

"Not a word. He'd clamp down on it pronto. C'mon, Mickey, the Dunster Funsters aren't licked yet."

That was how it began. For the best part of the next three days neither Mickey nor Derry Talbot nor Fog did much about their coming examinations. Of all this the Duke knew nothing. In fact his first suspicion of what was going on came when he opened the *Crimson* four mornings later and read a short notice on the front page.

"The name of James H. Wellington, Jr., of Waterloo, Iowa, captain of this year's track team, has been added to the list of nominations for marshal by petition." His heart jumped. Nominated . . . for marshal. Somewhere behind those cold, informal lines he felt Fog's hand. Here was a chance. If only he could get enough votes to edge into third place, everything would be saved and he could face his father with a smile on Class Day and Commencement.

The fun began. It was an election the like of which Harvard hadn't known for years, with managers, regular workers on each side, and a determined effort by both crowds to get out their vote and not be defeated. The marshals were chosen according to the number of votes, the man receiving the highest number becoming first marshal, the next two in line, second and third. There were six candidates in all besides the Duke, and his chances seemed none too good, for Mickey as football captain was sure of first place. That left the other two marshals to be disputed for by the Duke, Jack Parker, captain of a championship hockey team who'd had an offer from the Boston Bruins, Henry Davis, editor-in-chief of the *Crimson* and one of the most popular men in the class, Dave Sortwell, captain of the crew, who had never rowed on a losing eight in college, Spencer Morgan, the president of the Circle, and Alan Osgood, president of the Pudding and "Ibis" on the *Lampoon*. All of them belonged to the Circle which gave them its help in the election.

Campaign headquarters for the Duke was in Derry Talbot's room in Dunster. Fog, for one so imaginative, was curiously systematic, and leaving nothing to chance had divided the whole class into sections, with one of his workers assigned to each section. This man's job was to meet and talk on behalf of the Duke to every man in his section. The canvass was thorough and as election day approached it appeared from the response of the class that the Duke had a good chance for third place. The general opinion seemed to be that he had been treated unfairly in being left off the list of nominations for class officers. The *Crimson* never mentioned the stirring events going on around its front door, but by the eve of election the senior class and even the college was pretty well aroused. As for the Duke, he tried hard to be unconcerned about the events of the moment and failed utterly. Too much was at stake. If he became a marshal everything would be different; it would mean the success of his four years at Harvard and justification in the eyes of his father.

All this which Mickey had seen at the start, Fog began to appreciate. He also realized that the end of college was the end of an era in a man's life, the end of one struggle at hand and the start of another just ahead. That how his high-strung roommate went at that second and more important struggle would be determined by his last weeks at Cambridge which were to set the stamp of failure or success on his undergraduate life at Harvard.

Now Fog was in his element. Work was neglected for those next few days as he became again the cool and determined planner of the broadcast of the president's dinner at the Fly Club, the same ingenious Fog who had engineered the fake issue of the *Crimson* which the previous year had fooled the entire newspaper world. Everything was organized as in a regular political campaign down to watchers at the polls, for Fog knew well the adversaries who were against him. Finally election day rolled round.

Dunster and the other Houses and the whole

of Cambridge woke that morning to a dismally heavy rain beating on the roofs. Fog rose cursing while the Duke felt a sinking in his spirits. Rain had harried him at critical moments, first on the afternoon of the dual meet in New Haven, and now on this all-important day when just a few votes one way or the other might make all the difference. Rain hurt his chances because it would keep the commuters from voting. The commuters, also known colloquially as "meatballs," were the men who lived at home in Dorchester, Malden, Everett, or other suburbs, and commuted regularly to classes in cars or by the subway. They'd be likely to support the Duke because they were not in the Circle and because many of them knew him.

The rain continued. It increased as the day went along, but it failed to dampen interest in the election. For there had never been a class election like this. Janitors stood in the doorways discussing the Duke's chances, in the Coop, in Billings and Stover, in the cafeterias everyone was speculating on the result; even the barbers round the Square cut their clients' hair and talked about the election, while the one topic in dining rooms and commons was whether the Duke would cut the Circle vote enough to buck men like Davis and Sortwell and Osgood and edge into the list as third marshal. Had an injustice been done him? Some thought it had; others thought not. The whole college took sides and the oldest tutors in the Houses agreed they'd never seen anything like it. Men actually stood in line for twenty minutes or half an hour to vote in their Houses where the polling took place. Slowly, moving step by step, they filed in and stood before the tables.

"McAllister, J. C. Leverett, B-23."

"McAllister, J. C. Leverett, B-23. Check."

"Longstreth, W. B. H. Eliot, A-12."

"Longstreth, W. B. H. Eliot, A-12. Check."

"McCarthy, D. J., Jr. Lowell, F-54."

"McCarthy, D. J., Jr. Lowell, F-54. Check."

"Goldstein, M. 218 Hammond St., Roxbury."

"Goldstein, M. 218 Hammond, Roxbury. Check."

"Biddle, R. F. 2nd, Adams, G-32."

"Biddle, R. F. 2nd, Adams, G-32. Check."

So it went until long past the middle of the afternoon, name after name checked and re-checked and sometimes challenged by one side or the other. Dunster was expected to go strongly for the Duke because everyone knew him and House spirit was fairly strong. Autos banged through the Square bringing out the last tardy voters, even a few patients at Stillman Infirmary were rushed down to the polling booths, and all the while Fog stayed on the job, watching the voting, superintending his men, checking on the line that passed through. At four the polls were finally closed, the ballots tied up for counting, and he returned to the room for a brief moment to change his soggy clothes.

His face was serious as he entered. To be sure he said little, but the Duke knew him and realized from his attitude that he was worried. There were no jests, no wisecracks, and the Duke, whose hopes had been high during the day that he'd get enough votes to squeeze into third place, steeled himself to take the result as philosophically as he could. After all, old Jackson used to say that was what an education did for you, made you see things in their proper light. Mickey from his desk yelled at Fog tossing clothes round his bedroom.

"Well, all right, what about it? How'd we do? Everything okay? Or not? Tell us, will ya?"

"Yep, you did all right. Everyone did all right,

Mickey. I'm pushing off for the official count at the *Crimson* office now, and soon's I know anything I'll telephone."

"Yes, but how's it look? How are things, haven't you any idea at all?"

"Uhuh, I've got a fairly good idea, but you better wait. It's too early to be sure of anything. Just be ready for some surprises, that's all." And he was down the stairs and away. Surprises? Mickey looked at the Duke and the Duke looked at Mickey.

"What's he mean? Hey . . . Fog . . . wait a minute." But his footsteps echoed on the stone flags below. He was gone.

Six o'clock. By this time the sun had come out, and as Mickey and the Duke entered the dining room together his mind went back to that familiar spot the year before on the evening he'd won the race against Painton of Yale, and the tinkle of knives and forks on glasses, and how it warmed him and embarrassed him and made him happy. Why—say, it was starting again. Just a tinkle, a few more, a lot more, and now the whole room was at it. They must know something he didn't. Anyhow it was comforting to hear that sound once more, to listen to them shouting at him across the tables, but he knew nothing definitely about the result except that the House must have gone pretty solidly his way. After dinner he drifted up to the room with Mickey and men kept coming to congratulate him. Nothing was known yet. Seven thirty, eight o'clock, and still Fog didn't return. They tried to get him by telephone at eight thirty, but he wouldn't leave the room where the ballots were being counted.

Then their telephone rang at last. Mickey grabbed it. "Yes . . . well . . . what . . . sure he is . . . who wants to talk to him. . . . WHAT . . . he is . . . they did . . . your man said what . . . why, no, we don't even know ourselves yet . . . better call back later . . . 'bout half an hour, maybe an hour . . ." He set the telephone down. "Phew. Boston *Globe*. They want to know who is first marshal and get a picture, seems their correspondent here in Cambridge telephoned in that you and I were running neck and neck. . . ."

"Neck and neck?"

" 'S what he said. Neck and neck." The Duke couldn't believe it. Running neck and neck with Mickey. Then he was elected to something anyway. Things were all right. He was in, he was elected, he was a marshal, he'd won. . . .

"Here comes Fog." It was not Fog, it was Dave Sterry, his lieutenant, up to report to the crowd in the room. "Well, boys, here's the First Marshal of the class and I be darned if I know who to congratulate. There's half a dozen or more ballots invalidated that they're having a sweet old fight about. Seems several men connected with the class all through college are listed in the catalogue as unclassified instead of seniors because they lacked a half course or a course last fall. Question is are they eligible. Anyway you look it's a close thing. Last count was McGuire 212, Wellington 214. Your guess is as good as mine right now."

First Marshal. It went to his head, it stung him, it burned into his brain. He might be . . . but he thought of Mickey. The Irishman came over, his face aglow, shaking his head and extending his hand. "Why, hang it all, we ought never to have let you into this thing. Last week it was all in the bag. . . ."

To think that ten days before he'd been advising his family not to come East. First Marshal! The telephone rang. Fog, talking from the *Crim-*

son office, explained that so far as could be told, with a final counting still to come, the Duke was ahead by seven votes. Seven votes in five hundred and eighty men voting out of the class of six hundred and sixteen.

First Marshal. Captain of the track team and now First Marshal. Mickey had his arm round him as half of Dunster came storming up the stairs to find the man the class had just elected. There were men he'd known shyly and diffidently as a freshman, better as sophomores, intimately as juniors and seniors when they became friendly, familiar faces. Men he'd eaten with day after day for three long years, worked with on Soldier's Field, sat beside at classes in Sever or Emerson, a few commuters to whom he'd been friendly for no reason except that he felt sorry for them. They were all there, all grabbing for his hand. Now the room resounded to shouts and yells and someone was bringing up beer and they were yelling his name out from opened windows across the way.

Meanwhile Mickey was happier than if he had been made First Marshal himself. And just as surprised as anyone at the result. The Duke couldn't speak, he couldn't say anything because he wanted to shout, to yell, to call his family by telephone and make sure those plans hadn't been changed. Captain of the track team. Intercollegiate two-mile record-holder. Now First Marshal of the Class. Only his degree remained. Get it? Of course he would. Oh, boy, bring on those Olympic trials.

9

Those last three days were passed in a dizzy haze. Afterward he remembered them as blurred movement. It was a haze caused by rush and hurry, not by the heat of mid-July in New York.

First there was his passport. As he hoped to travel a little in France and England afterward a passport was necessary. This complicated business demanded a trip to lower Manhattan, the filling out of forms, signing and witnessing of his name, the taking of photographs. There were visas to be obtained. Last minute purchases. Could toothpaste be obtained abroad? Some said no, others yes; the Duke was taking no chances. There were wires home. Worst of all were the hours at headquarters in the hotel; hours of standing in line. In one room you lined up for the Handbook which contained a letter of congratulation from the President of the Olympic Committee, a general statement of the responsibility of every member of the team for his conduct, a list of the various teams and their managers, an application for leave of absence afterward which he had to fill out and sign, a quartermaster's receipt for his clothes which he hadn't obtained, and a release, also to be signed. It was complicated, this Handbook, and took time to read. Then in another room he stood in line for his Identification Card; the Card which was to furnish admission to the Olympic Village and the Stadium in Berlin. By this time he really began to feel he was a member of the team. Last of all there were hours of standing in line to be measured for his uniform.

The Handbook brought home to everyone that this was no ordinary trip. If that didn't, the celebrities round the hotel did. All through the suite of the Olympic Committee, standing in the long lines in various rooms, in the lobby and the halls and the elevators, were famous figures who once were names to the Duke. Now they were human beings, personalities. There was Ace Monahan, Notre Dame all-America and hurdling star, Al Jefferson, the big Negro sprinter from the West, Mike Hanney, the Chicago cop and shot-put champion of three Olympics, Davison of Southern California, who pole-vaulted higher than any living person, besides one or two men he'd known from running in the Olympic trials, like Schumacher who vaguely remembered the Duke and nodded politely if not enthusiastically. Best of all there was Harry Painton, a friend. Like himself, Harry had made the team by a hair.

The morning of their departure came in a feverish whirl of excitement. He slept little the night before; the noise of New York traffic, worse even than the traffic round the freshman dormitories in the Yard, kept him awake. At nine thirty they gathered in the lobby of the hotel while a cordon of mounted policemen held the gaping crowd back, and piled into buses for the trip across town. There was considerable delay but finally with the sirens of the motorcycle men up front screeching, they raced over to the docks. Only then could the Duke realize it. Yep, he was really going to the Olympic Games.

What did it matter if he was the most insignificant member of the big party? If he knew no one, if Harry Painton was his only friend. No matter if he had squeezed in by inches with a third place in the final tryouts. He was going to Berlin. To the Olympic Games.

There was a yell and a cheer as they drew near the docks and, stopping, piled from the long line of buses. There beside the pier was the ship covered with flags and bunting, and as they went aboard the excitement in the air was intense. The Duke had never felt anything like it, even before a big race. He and Harry found their room, a small inside cabin with two bunks down tourist class. "Not so good for a couple of long-legged gentlemen," remarked Harry. "However, I guess we'll manage." The Duke didn't care. He was aboard and that was all that mattered.

Harry's family soon rolled in to see him off. They filled and overfilled the little room, so the

Duke wandered up on deck to find out what was going on. Impossible not to feel exhilarated and lighthearted in the noisy atmosphere. On deck there was more excitement. A sailor was raising the Olympic flag to the mast; five colored circles entwined on a background of white. Unable to see over the crowd, he went up to an upper deck where, edging to the rail, he could look down upon the ceremony below.

Newsreel machines were grinding away, Olympic officials, their straw hats in their hands, were declaiming, and the flag was being raised in a terrific din when he was shoved violently by a large individual with a movie camera trying to get a picture. So oblivious was the intruder to everything but his picture that he had squeezed a girl next to the Duke back from the rail where she could see nothing.

"Here, have my place." She was nice looking, dark hair, slender, a passenger evidently and not a member of the team. The Olympic girl athletes were hardly figures to be mistaken. She straightened her hat which had been shaken to one side, and smiled, shaking her head.

"Thanks. The thing's over anyhow. Nothing much to see." In the midst of the general excitement she was calm, and it was plain she was not sailing to Berlin for the Games. Then she jumped. So too did the Duke. It was the piercing whistle of the steamer pulling away from the pier. "All ashore that's a-going ashore," laughed someone. The whistle started again, stopped, and resumed its shriek.

"Well, here we go." No wonder she wasn't moved and steamed up. She wasn't on the team. She hadn't fought to get aboard that ship as every single athlete had fought, through meets like the Intercollegiates, through the big final tryouts against dozens, hundreds, of other good men. She was probably just a passenger, not even her first trip, probably. "Here we go." The whistle gave a final, furious blast. Down below the rails were jammed with boys waving good-bye to the crowded pier. As they edged into the stream the pierhead was black with people all thrusting flags at them. But she took it calmly. In fact he saw she was looking at him closely.

"What's that?" He missed her question in the shouting and din.

"I said . . . aren't you Wellington . . . the runner?"

A nice glow came over him, subduing the

slightly lonely feeling that he had no friend, no relative on the pier waving good-bye and wishing him luck. He was pleased. Who wouldn't be? He was more than pleased, he was a little astonished that the girl should have known him. Especially as he really hadn't run a first class race that year. He nodded.

"Thought so. I saw you last spring in the Intercollegiates."

"Oh." He was blushing. "You mean a year ago . . ." The time he'd won from Harry Painton and set the record. When anyone mentioned that race they usually went into superlatives which made him somewhat uneasy. She was simple and different. Yet there was much more in the one sentence and the inquiring look than in the usual words of sloppy praise. They warmed him. This was the first time since his arrival in New York that anyone except Harry had known who he was.

Now the steamer was drawing away from the side of the pier, now slowly turning in midstream. Bands were playing. The sun was no longer hot, only pleasantly warm. Flags stood out in the breeze on the masts, on the pierheads, even on the little tugs below. He looked at her again. She didn't exactly look like a member of the team, for many of the girls who ran and jumped were large, uncouth, and sometimes noisy females. Yet she had an athletic figure; tall with long, strong hands. Then someone passed before them, a tall figure who turned and stood there. The Duke became conscious someone was looking at him, and he heard that voice, the same friendly quiet voice.

"Well, Duke!"

"Slips!" The Duke held out his arms. Slips on board! Now everything was set. The Olympics, with Slips Ellis. He hardly dared hope, dared ask his friend.

"You . . . you aren't going along, too, on the team I mean, Slips?"

"Sure am. Assistant to old Sanderson, the head coach. I knew you'd got on and I'm certainly glad you made it, boy."

"Only just, Slips. A third place in the 1,500 meters, by inches, too. That's all that saved my skin. Anyhow I'm here and you're here, too. Isn't it great? Naturally I don't expect to do much over there . . . but the trip, you know. . . ."

The girl had vanished. With Slips' arm in the Duke's they walked down the deck. "Don't talk like that. You remember I never allowed it. Of course you'll do well. Now tell me about everything, the whole year since I left Cambridge. First of all, how'd you happen to run the 1,500 meters. I should have entered you in the 5,000."

They found a quiet place in the stern away from the bustle and pushing mob, and while the skyline of Manhattan got lower and lower on the horizon, the Duke told his friend the story of that disastrous year—the Studebaker Mile, the Yale meet and the Intercollegiates, how he chose the 1,500 because there were so many good distance men in the 5,000 that, had he run, Harry Painton would have been shut out and failed to make the team. So he ran the 1,500 and barely edged in himself, as Slips pointed out with that familiar shake of his head, a risky thing to do. His arm rested affectionately on the Duke's knee. Now everything was all right, Slips was there. And while New York faded into the summer haze, he told his story in turn, of eight months looking in vain for a coaching job in the colleges.

The Duke went to sleep happy that night. The next morning he woke to a queer, uneasy movement. The boat. It was not steady and to anyone from as far inland as Iowa, most unpleasant.

Harry wasn't happy either and they dressed hurriedly and went down to breakfast. He felt better as the day went along. Some calisthenics on the boat deck and a few laps round the promenade deck before lunch helped, and to his surprise he ate a good meal. After lunch Harry called to him in the main hall.

"Hey, Duke . . . c'mon down. Our uniforms are here."

There they were. Two large boxes, one on each bunk. They opened them and found the complete Olympic uniform. The Duke took each garment tenderly out of the covering and laid it down on the bed, first a double-breasted blue serge coat with a red, white, and blue shield on the pocket, and a pair of white flannel trousers for formal occasions. Then a white shirt with a red, white, and blue necktie. A white pullover sweater. A red sweater with a black USA on the front. And then his track suit: white satin trunks with an elastic ribbon for a belt in the top and red, white, and blue pipings down the sides, and a white running shirt with a tri-colored sash across the breast.

He looked at them as they lay fresh and new spread out before him. He was really a member of the Olympic team, he, Duke Wellington, of Waterloo, Iowa. Really going to Europe. No doubt about it now. He fingered the running trunks. The stuffy stateroom faded, he smelled the fresh summer breeze, felt the sun on his bare back, now the cinders from the man ahead spattered on his legs and he heard the sluff-sluff-sluff of footsteps on the track in the great stadium in Berlin.

10

"Duke, come up to the first class smoking room tonight before dinner. Got a friend wants to meet you."

It was the third day. Faces were sorting themselves out; members of the team of whom almost four hundred were aboard, managers, officials, trainers, coaches, newspapermen, and radio announcers.

"Me? What's he want to meet me for?"

"It's a girl. Think she met you or saw you run

once or something. One of our fencers and a good one, too."

That made two persons aboard who'd seen him run. There was that girl he met the day they sailed who had since vanished, or at least the boat was so big and there were so many people milling around the decks and through the corridors that he had missed her. When he plowed through the crowded first class smoking room that evening, however, he saw her sitting in a corner with Slips.

"Look here . . . you never told me you were a fencer, and on the Olympic team."

"You never asked me."

"She is. And an important member. In fact a point winner; you're both point winners I'm counting upon."

"Who? Me? What, with Schumacher, and that whoosit, that Englishman . . ."

"You mean Brocklehurst? I expect you to handle him, Duke."

"And the German, too? Not a chance, Slips."

"I see. Just along for the ride." She shot a glance at Slips Ellis which stung him.

"Of course not. I'll give everything, but I don't expect much luck. This is the Olympics in Berlin, not the Intercollegiates in the United States.

And look at my event. Now take the 5,000 meter run, for instance . . ."

Slips leaned over and patted his hand. He smiled. "Duke, every runner has talked that way about his event since the beginning of time. Harry Painton has those Finns, and they're very awkward customers. Now forget all that. Take it as just another race. Oh . . . hullo there, Mac." He nodded across the room. "Some interesting folks on this ship. That big man over there at that table, the bald-headed fellow laughing, that's Maguire, the Notre Dame football coach, the famous Doc Maguire. He's taking a crowd over for the Games. Man at his right is Casey, the sports columnist, and the other side is Jeff Crane from Stanford, the broad jumper."

Everyone was talking and laughter filled the room. The place was a scene of merriment. Slips continued. "In some ways this trip over is best. I remember the last Olympics over across. You see they've all made the team and there's a chance to relax and forget things a little. Take it easy for a few days. Say, I heard a funny one at lunch. Seems one of the men at our table is a marathon runner from the West. His twin brother wanted to come along and see him run the worst way, but there wasn't any money in the family. The boys at his office knew this so they took up a collection, raised four hundred bucks, the boss gave him a month's vacation, and he's coming over third class on the *Normandie* next week. When they told him about it he broke down and cried."

Slips rose quickly. "Excuse me. Just say a word to Harry." He went across the room to another table where he was greeted boisterously. The Duke never felt happier. He had made the Olympic team and was headed for a new adventure aided and helped by a man he loved. And across the table was an attractive girl who was an athlete and yet didn't look like most of the athletes aboard, a girl who had seen him run his best race of all. Which didn't hurt, either.

"How do you happen to know Slips Ellis?"

"Slips? Why, he comes from my home, Muskegon, Michigan. Then he married a cousin of mine, Ruth Grimes. He's all right, isn't he?"

"You bet he's all right. Say, I know her, Mrs. Ellis. She's nice. Wish I could tell you what it meant to us at Cambridge to lose him this year. Made an awful lot of difference to some of us." The Duke turned on her, face aglow. If she liked Slips she must be all right.

"Uhuh. He got rather a raw deal there, didn't he? I heard all sorts of stories; of course he won't talk about it and Ruth won't, either."

"I should say he did." There was emphasis in his voice and he wanted to go on, but loyalty to Harvard stopped him. Was it loyalty to Harvard? He hesitated, wondering whether he was being loyal to Harvard, to an ideal, to an athletic director named Henry Horton, or just simply being foolish. A perplexing question. He wasn't sure of the answer.

"Everyone loved him at Michigan. You know he was there five years before going East. We all wondered . . ."

"Well, everyone loved him at Cambridge, too. Nearly everyone, that is." He couldn't say much. The situation still hurt. "What's he going to do now? I gathered he hasn't landed a place yet."

"No. That's just it. You know how hard it is to get college jobs. Then he was let out so suddenly. Ernest Brewer, the head of the A.A.U., is an old Michigan man and knew Slips in college. I think he got him this job as assistant to Sanderson so he'd meet some of the athletic directors and people. You know . . ."

Yes, he knew. The thought of Slips out of a

job wasn't pleasant. Once again he saw the two-family frame house in North Cambridge, heard the click of the door latch and the voice of Slips' wife, this girl's cousin, calling down to him. And once again he saw the weavings and interlockings of the athletic business, a business which suddenly raised men to positions of responsibility and for no good reason as suddenly tossed them out. The girl was talking.

"It isn't as if he wasn't a good coach. We all know he's a good . . ."

"Not as well as I do." The Duke was so vehement that she looked at him quickly. "Let me tell you I shouldn't be here now except for that man over there. You bet he's a good coach. And a good friend, too." He shut up. It was difficult to say much about Slips to strangers, even those who knew and loved him.

"If he hadn't made a good record at Harvard. But he had a championship team last year, didn't he? And this year it wasn't so hot, was it?"

The Duke winced. That hurt. But facts were facts. "No, it wasn't so hot." She noticed his subdued tone.

"Sorry. I forgot you were the captain. But after all it's the coach who really counts in sports today. You know that."

"Maybe. The captain can't shake off his share of responsibility. There are good captains and bad, like coaches."

"You can't fool me. My brother was football captain at Michigan. I know just how much captains count in intercollegiate sport the way things are set up nowadays." She spoke with conviction. She was right about football as Mickey so often said; was she right about track? Did the coach have complete power? Some coaches, yes, others like Slips, no. Before he could answer, the blond head of Harry Painton came into sight. The Duke reached out and grabbed his sleeve as he passed their table.

"My roommate. Harry Painton of Yale, running in the 5,000 meters. Miss . . . Miss . . ."

"Davis. Helen Davis."

"You remember Harry. He was the man I had that terrific finish with in the two miles in the Intercollegiates last year." She nodded vaguely, and the Duke was not unhappy to observe that she only recalled the winner of that race. Harry observed it, also.

"You may have forgotten that finish, but I haven't. Wrung me out for six months, and I feel it in my old bones right now. Say, Duke . . ." He leaned over the table. "That lad I was telling you about, the one I beat for third place in the tryouts, Mac something-or-other. From Texas, he was, the chap who didn't qualify. Well, he signed on as a stoker and is coming on the ship that way . . ." Someone at the next table pulled him over. Harry knew everyone aboard.

"Yes, and I believe there's a girl who just failed to make the swimming team on board as a stewardess. You know, I'm not so sure I want to come bad enough for that."

The Duke was surprised. "You wouldn't? Mean to say you didn't want to make the team?"

"Oh, I wanted to make the team all right. But that bad . . . I don't honestly know. As for the United States winning, it doesn't seem to me so very important in spite of all these speeches we have by the officials every morning. 'Fight talks,' as the boys call 'em."

Again he was shocked. It was a sour note in his enthusiastic mood. A sort of feminine Fog, that's what this girl was.

"Yes, I like to win and all that. But principally I love fencing. I like to fence. That's where we have it all over you people. You have to stop when these Games are over; we can go on all our life enjoying fencing."

"Me, too. Me, too. Think I'm gonna shut up

shop because I'm through college? I hope to get a job teaching in a boys' school and coaching track, that's what I want to do more than anything. I'd like to, well, sort of go on and do what Slips does, you know. And if I get a job it'll give me time to run and a chance to train. No, sir! You see a runner has just so much in him. I started late and have only been running a few years, so why shouldn't I keep at it a while yet?"

"Do you think you will?" She looked at him. "I don't."

There was something disquieting in her voice. It made him uneasy. "Why not?"

"For several reasons. First of all you're an idealist. That's easy to see. And sooner or later you'll run up against the system that threw Slips Ellis out of Harvard for no particular reason at all. You wait, you'll see. There's another reason. It's impossible just to go out and run the way we fence every day. To run you must train, you must work, and I suppose you must suffer. Anyone who fences gets fun and pleasure and exercise without that."

He was confused and a little worried, because vaguely he saw what she was trying to say. "But I love running as much as you love fencing."

"There's a difference. You'll find out later.

Well, anyhow, it's great fun to be along. I'm looking forward to seeing Germany, to knowing the place and the people. I want to try to find out for myself what makes this man Hitler tick." She expressed herself queerly, and the more he saw of her the more she reminded him of Fog his roommate. But she was interesting. He himself had hardly thought of Germany and Hitler in the excitement of competing in the Games.

By the time they reached the Channel he'd seen a good deal of her. The *Manhattan* sailed past the white cliffs of Dover on the English shore, through shipping large and small, every vessel dipping its ensign to the Olympic emblem. When they saw the haze on the horizon which meant Germany he had decided this girl was the most interesting person aboard. She could be depended on to have original views on everything: the Games, the athletes aboard, the managers, and especially the women managers. Before the end, however, she too had been caught by the contagion of excitement in the air. No wonder, for on the last day their training routine was completely disrupted. Meetings of each team were held, instructions issued for their arrival in Hamburg, and orders given for costumes and other things. Meanwhile a rumor spread round, as only rumors can aboard ship, that the customs examination at Hamburg where they would land would be perfunctory. Inside of three hours the entire bar was stripped of cigarettes and tobacco.

There was baggage to pack, and soon the halls became mountains of suitcases, mostly bulging and tied with rope, because everyone had the regulation uniform to jam into bags already over-filled. There were the usual number of passports tucked away in valises that had to be unearthed from piles of luggage; but by late afternoon everyone was ready to land. Then, with the shore in sight, word came that the steamer was slowing down so it could sail up the River Elbe in the evening, with debarkation set for the next morning.

Like everyone the Duke wondered just what kind of a reception they would have, and how the Germans would feel toward them. After dinner he went up to the boat deck with Helen Davis to watch the ship glide through the clean, smooth water. It was eight-thirty but still daylight, and they could plainly see people on both banks of the wide estuary. Everything appeared strange to him, the absence of automobiles, the large number of bicycles, the queer people on the banks greeting them with outstretched arms. It was the first time either of them had seen the Hitler salute which for the next three weeks was to be so much a part of their daily life.

Darkness did not fall for over an hour. By this time the river had narrowed somewhat. Overhead between the masts the searchlights played on the Stars and Stripes and the Olympic ensign, while toots and whistles came to them from the shore and from passing river steamers. A Hamburg-American liner outward bound raced past the *Manhattan*, dipping its flag, passengers jamming the decks and waving. Even Helen, who had been to Europe before, was caught by the emotion of the moment, the calm river, the lights ashore, the shouting and noise from the banks and passing craft.

"Look. Look over there!" The river became still narrower and they could see the banks plainly in the late twilight. It gave the scene a kind of unreal, theatrical quality, for each side was lined with small cafés, and tiny beer gardens set in flowered arbors. Everywhere the people stood with arms extended, shouting.

"What's that? What are they saying?" She listened carefully.

"Heil. They're welcoming us. It's a kind of greeting. Heil. Hear them . . ."

Through the warm summer night came the sound from the shores, plain, unmistakable. *"Heil, Amerika, Heil."* And from the deck below the deep-throated roars of hundreds of young Americans answered them back. All the way up the river, as it slowly narrowed, there was this exchange, until at last the lights of the big city rose ahead and the crowds on the shore became denser.

"Heil, Amerika, Heil . . . Heil. . . ."

It was after eleven o'clock and the boat was dropping anchor opposite the pier when coaches and trainers came to push their excited charges to bed. From the little excursion boats, from launches and rowboats, and from the shore cheers and greetings echoed up and down the stream.

There was little sleep aboard the *Manhattan* that night.

11

W elcome to Germany," said the sign on the pier just above the gangplank where the team debarked at eight the next morning. On one side of the sign was the American flag. On the other the German swastika, black in a white circle. It was the first time the Duke had seen that emblem which was to be so much in evidence during the next three weeks.

Once on the pier, the rumor of the previous afternoon proved entirely correct. There were no customs examinations for the athletes and all American baggage, cigarettes included, was despatched straight on to Berlin.

The Duke looked back along the line as they filed slowly off the pier headed by a band. Impossible not to feel stirred, not to have a touch of pride at being an American in this foreign land, part of an American team, stared at by the curious but friendly faces of the few onlookers permitted on the dock early that morning. The line stretched back as far as he could distinguish; everyone in a straw hat, blue serge suit with the colored American shield, and everybody wearing the striped American necktie. Ahead the band was blaring out "The Stars and Stripes Forever," as they moved to the street where an enormous crowd yelled greetings. It sounded like a genuine welcome.

Piling into buses they drove through an avenue of American flags. "Where we goin', boys?" asked someone. "The Rathaus," said a voice up front. The City Hall, that's what it was, and the mayor, called a burgomeister in Germany, greeted them, tendered some American official the keys to the city, and wine was served. It was better even than the stuff served at the Pudding Spread on Class Day. The Duke liked it. Then back to the station where two special trains were waiting to take them to Berlin. Each one was marked *Der Fliegende Hamburger*. The Flying Hamburger. That much German he could read, but he wished he'd spent more time on the language in college, and already he envied the few men around him who could exchange quips with the bystanders. Getting into a crowded compartment, he was hardly seated when the train moved noiselessly out of the station through a forest of stretched hands along the packed platforms.

The countryside was flat, clean, and not especially interesting, but it was new and different and everyone looked out eagerly, although the Duke felt dizzy from new impressions and emotions. They evidently had the right of way, and at every station their engine tooted proudly as if they were royalty. Indeed they might have been royalty, for on every platform and even along the track soldiers in iron helmets were drawn up at Present Arms. The whole compartment was impressed and the whole compartment said so.

"Certainly glad to have us. And you sure see lots of soldiers in this man's country," someone remarked.

"Yeah. There was a bunch of army officers on the pier handshaking the badgers when we came off." This term was the expression commonly used by the team to designate the officials; the men who wore badges, the members of the Olympic Committee of whom there seemed to be almost twice as many as competitors. That had also struck the Duke on landing. A soldier in uniform was something you seldom saw at home. Here it seemed as if every other male wore a uniform of one sort or another.

Uniforms and flags. "They sure are patriotic, these folks," remarked the man next to him, as they whizzed through a town completely covered with the gold and black swastika. He'd noticed that, too, everywhere the swastika. These flags and uniforms everywhere didn't somehow fit with the kind, friendly faces of the natives. The Duke thought he'd never seen so many smiles as he had since leaving the *Manhattan* two hours before. It seemed as if no one smiled at home.

Berlin at last. There were crowds in the station held back by ropes in the hands of uniformed men, Storm Troopers, someone said they were, though just what that meant he wasn't certain. Another celebration took place beside the big engine covered with a swastika, at which German dignitaries in top hats presented armfuls of flowers to the American badgers, and plump blonde fräuleins in the crowd waved at the men on the team who waved back. Then they were formed in line and again the Duke found himself near the head. The order was given and the column moved slowly outdoors.

Even the big hammer thrower up front was staggered. A thousand, ten thousand persons were jammed into the square, arms uplifted, mouths open, shouting. A band bigger than the Harvard band, bigger even than the Indiana band which was the largest the Duke had ever seen, was lost in the tumult. They went toward the waiting buses drawn up at the far end of the square, and as the head of the line reached the first bus, they paused, waiting for the order to climb aboard. All this time the yelling continued. The hammer thrower grinned and taking off his hat waved it to the crowd. More noise. Beside him was a tiny Berlin policeman. He reached down, removed the cop's helmet, put it on his head and clapped his own straw hat with its colored ribbon on the head of the bewildered policeman.

The crowd loved it. They liked the big blond Californian giant, they enjoyed his joke, they roared as he stood looking foolish with a steel helmet several sizes too small on his head. They shouted guttural greetings which unfortunately meant nothing to the Duke. Yet their delight was apparent enough, their friendly faces, their broad smiles told of their good-humored enjoyment. He remembered the anti-German leaflets which had been scattered through everyone's stateroom as the boat left New York, and instantly he became annoyed. This was a decent and kindly people and he liked them.

Through the roaring mob to the Rathaus in buses. The tops were rolled back and the trip was a procession of triumph. How many persons stood in the flag-bedecked streets he couldn't guess; half a million, a million maybe, more people anyway than the Duke had ever seen gathered together in one place before. From iron balconies high up on the highest houses, from roofs, windows, and from every cornice they were cheering. Overhead a majestic Zeppelin moved gracefully. The team was impressed and even the most flippant was awed and silent.

"Some town, hey, buddy!" said the man next to him. The Duke, too moved to speak, nodded. Yes, it was some town all right.

At the City Hall the Mayor read a short greeting in clipped, precise English, and then as they emerged and boarded the buses again for the final trip of the day the roar assaulted them once more. Berlin was in holiday mood. The streets were a mass of banners and flags of every nation, garlands hung from the electric light posts, on every corner was a plaque with the coat of arms of some nation, and everywhere and on all sides the encircled banner of the Olympic Games and the swastika of the Third Reich. Yes, these folks knew how to do things. Gradually they moved into the suburbs and so out toward the Stadium, still through cheering crowds. A lane of troops, a kind of guard of honor, lined both sides of the roads, standing shoulder to shoulder all the way to their destination ten miles from the heart of the city. And along their path behind those troops were cheering, friendly thousands. Somebody said they'd been waiting on the sidewalks since daybreak.

Through that path of noise the buses moved on to the Olympic Village where all the teams of all nations were quartered. They disembarked for more ceremonies, more heel-clickings by men in top hats, more handshakes by the German Olympic officials and army officers in their trim, gray-green uniforms. With the badgers up front flanked by the German officers, they moved under an archway and into the Village, past small white houses with red roofs in pine groves, their home for the period of the games.

The Duke was assigned to a house where he and Harry Painton were to share a room. English-speaking attendants directed them to their quarters which they soon found. Inside, carefully sorted and placed at separate ends of the little room, was their baggage waiting for them. The two Americans were impressed. They thought their stay in New York and the experience of the trip across had taught them something about organization, but these people were masters at that game as they were to discover later.

12

To be sure he'd never seen many big stadiums. There was his own familiar and beloved one at Cambridge, there was the Bowl at New Haven, and once he'd driven with his father from Waterloo to see Minnesota play a Conference game at Minneapolis. But he was sure there was never anything like the Olympic stadium, that huge pile of granite looking as if built to stand a thousand years.

It seated over a hundred thousand spectators

in two decks, and was surrounded by an athletic layout so complete that even the badgers of the American team were speechless. There was a swimming pool with bleachers for twenty thousand, fields for hockey, polo, soccer, tennis courts, gymnasiums, two excellent practice tracks, restaurants, and several stations at different ends of the grounds for both the underground and railway trains to Berlin.

The American team reached the scene about one week before the start, a period in which the Duke applied himself earnestly to the business of getting back a form which had more or less deserted him since the day Slips Ellis left Cambridge. He was older, more experienced, a better tactical runner, but he knew he wasn't as fast as he had been the year before. He felt convinced, however, that under Slips' eyes in those two workouts a day, he soon would be. Slips could do it. So the Duke trained faithfully, and before long noticed the precious and intangible thing, form, coming back. There was a lift, a joy in his running which had not been there for a long while. Once in the afternoon he wandered over to the gymnasium to watch Helen practice; but she had finished so he walked back with her to the Friesenhaus, the dormitory for women athletes. This was almost the only time he saw her before the Games began, for he was busy and no women were admitted to the Olympic Village, in fact wherever you went it was necessary to show your Identification Card.

The weather was none too warm, but each day he felt better. And each day he saw real progress. With Slips there to watch and correct the little errors of form and timing which his anxiety and concentration on the job of being captain had allowed to crop out, he realized happily he was coming back. Running was fun again. He threw back his head every morning on the track, jumped up and down just for the sheer joy of being carefree again; it was like the old days when he was just a simple candidate for the track team at Harvard with no hope of ever becoming a real runner. Even the strenuous setting-up exercises, the bending and dipping and twisting which all the track men took daily, failed to cool his enthusiasm. He was slowly working into shape. The track and field events started the first week of the Games, but he knew that if he continued to develop his finishing sprint he would place in one heat anyhow and so qualify for the finals.

The day of the opening ceremonies was gray but not stormy. In full Olympic uniform, straw hat, striped red, white, and blue necktie, blue serge coat and flannel trousers, the whole American team was drawn up on the parade ground of the *Reichssportfeld* outside the Stadium waiting to take their place in the procession. Promptly at four o'clock, the hour set, an enormous roar came to them from inside. These people did things on time. It was four and Hitler was entering the enclosure.

Before the Americans passed the entire parade. Each nation had a standard bearer with the name of his country, followed by another bearer holding the national colors. To Greece, originator of the Olympics of old, went the place of honor. Then came a series of small nations: Argentina, Brazil, Bolivia, 250 Frenchmen in berets, blue coats, and white trousers. The English followed in much the same costume as the Americans, and shortly after came an enormous crowd of Japanese, so many they appeared to have the largest team in the Games. There were Egyptians in red fezzes, Italians in black caps and black shirts, Indians in turbans, Norwegians, Portuguese, until finally the signal was given and the Americans swung into the procession. Eight abreast they moved along to enter the Stadium.

This moment he would never forget. A hundred thousand persons stood cheering as the team walked round the track, the American flag at its head, and finally passed the box where Hitler was standing with three officers in uniform, their caps over their eyes, and an elderly man who was completely bald and shaved on the head in the German fashion. Luckily the Duke was at the end of the line, and as the men came past they placed their hats over their hearts and turned their heads to the reviewing stand. There was Hitler, with the little mustache, looking down at the marching Americans. They went along and replaced their straw hats when past him.

"Just like his pictures," murmured the Duke. It was a stupid remark and he realized it.

"Well, Foolish, what'd you expect him to look like, Paul Whiteman?" replied Harry. The Duke's reply was cut short by a roar. It was a roar the like of which he'd never heard before.

The Stadium, the entire Stadium of a hundred and ten thousand men and women, was on its feet, arms extended, shouting. It was not a shriek nor yet a yell, but a deep-seated, passionate roar, a sound almost terrifying in its tone to the Duke. Then they burst into song, in unison they sang, and when they finished they sang again in the same full-throated tone. Meanwhile the Americans marching below had drawn up before the Hitler box. Behind them five hundred German athletes in white suits and white yachting caps held out their arms to the little man in the box above.

Round the Stadium the last of the Germans were marching, the roaring continuous. Finally they, too, lined up with the athletes of the other nations and the ceremonies began. The bald-headed man beside Hitler, the President of the Games, spoke briefly, and then Hitler himself leaned into the microphone. His sentences were short, but every word had a bite. For the first time the Duke had a vision of the strength and power of this little man in uniform. There was something about him that made one uneasy. Now the Games were open.

A fanfare of trumpets. Then the noise of guns from without; eleven shots for the 11th Olympiade. Slowly the Olympic flag was raised to the central mast, while from the ramparts of the Stadium a hundred flags of the various participating nations rose, and at the same time several thousand doves released from the ground flew fluttering into the sky.

Then with perfect timing a dramatic incident occurred. One section of seats at the far end of the structure was vacant. Poised against the top stood an athlete in white running shirt and trousers, in his right hand a flaming torch. He was the last of thousands who had borne that lighted beacon all the way from Greece, through central Europe to Berlin. He ran lightly down the seats to the track, over the grass and, leaving behind a trail of bluish smoke, raced up the opposite end of the Stadium to a kind of brazier high in plain sight of the crowd. Applying the torch to the brazier he kindled the Olympic flame. The flames twisted and turned in the breeze. They were to burn like that for the duration of the Games.

The flagbearers formed a semicircle before the athletes, facing the committee box, and a big blond German stepped onto a small platform and took the Olympic oath. The Duke listened, as the German with the black eagle on his breast slowly and solemnly repeated the oath of the Olympics before those silent thousands. But impressed though he was, all the while the Duke in the front row of the American team was watching with a peculiar fascination the German Chancellor in his box. Throughout the ceremonies, which lasted over half an hour, he noticed that the Fuehrer kept nervously stroking his knees, a gesture which never ceased.

13

"Helen's won her preliminary round, Duke. She goes into the semifinals day after to-morrow." Slips came into the little room in the Olympic Village late the afternoon of the second day. "We thought we might all celebrate by going over to the baseball game in the Stadium to-night."

Harry Painton from his bed tossed a magazine to the floor. The Duke laid aside a letter he was writing home with some relief, for his ideas about

Germany and the Games were so confused that he found them difficult to put on paper.

"Baseball in the Olympics? That's like skating in Hawaii. Whoever thought up that one?" asked Harry. "I didn't know the Germans played baseball."

"No more they do. I don't have any idea why they are staging this game except to sell it to the natives. Seems they brought two American nines along and they give an exhibition tonight, that's about all I know. Be ready at seven fifteen."

Ready they were, and the party by that time had grown. Besides Slips and Helen and Harry and the Duke, Jim Casey, the sportswriter, and Cutler, the radio announcer, came along, too. The Duke was glad to meet these celebrities, and he especially wanted to see whether Casey was as quick and amusing in person as in print. It was soon evident to him that Casey knew his stuff, for in the short walk over to the Stadium between Slips and the columnist, the Duke began to get some real picture of the vastness of the enterprise and the organizing genius behind it all.

"Man who helped run our Games in L. A. tells

me they've simply taken over our plans and improved on everything we did. This plant, now, cost sixty millions."

"Dollars or marks?" asked Slips. Yes, there was a difference, wasn't there? The Duke could never keep it straight. Four, no, five, marks to the dollar.

"No, dollars, not marks. Sixty millions of dollars. Sure, they hope to get lots of it back through tourist trade and the crowd at the Games, but lots of it is in permanent improvements. And they've staged about the best show of its kind I've ever seen. Sixteen special trains a day from all parts of Germany, and cheap, too; they travel for a cent a mile round trip. How's that? Why, they even sold three million and a half tickets to the Games before the opening day."

"How much do tickets cost, anyhow?" This interested the Duke. How much did those quiet, nice people that he saw pouring into the Stadium or sitting on the ground eating sausages and rolls pay for admittance?

"Fifteen bucks apiece on the opening day. *And* no free list. Hey, Slips? We had a terrible time getting him in because there weren't enough invitations to go round for the badgers and managers and coaches attached to our various teams. Season tickets which let you in to everything cost forty dollars, twenty-four or sixteen, depending on location."

"That's for the whole period of the Games?"

"Yep, everything. Seats for the track and field events in the Stadium only are sixteen, twelve, with standing room at eight bucks." The Duke was dazzled by the accuracy of the man and his command of detail. There didn't seem to be anything he had missed. "I believe single day seats on big days are twenty marks, that's, less see . . . twenty marks, times . . . that makes about four eighty, and two forty or ten marks on ordinary days."

"What's the difference?"

"Well, the opening day was a big day; yesterday with shot-put and pole vault trials and so forth was an ordinary day."

"And they fill the Stadium?"

Casey turned on him. The Duke felt as if he'd said the wrong thing for there was immense scorn in the tones of the older man. "Fill it! Fill it! Say, boy, they filled this place three times in the first twenty-four hours. For the opening ceremonies, that was your little show in the afternoon, then in the evening for the *Hitlerjugend* festival, the Hitler Youth Movement, and finally yesterday afternoon on the first day of competition. That's three hundred and thirty thousand and a few more at an average of two forty a seat; pretty good, hey?" Easy to see that Mr. Casey was an admirer of German organizing talent and he succeeded in communicating his admiration to the Duke.

"Pretty good is right."

"Yes, and let me tell you another thing." His tone was admonishing and the Duke felt like a schoolboy in a classroom. "These babies don't stand any nonsense. No, sirree. Heard what happened yesterday in our place? Heard that, Slips? No?" Now what was coming! This man knew everything. The Duke edged in closer to lose nothing as he talked to Slips. "Why, it appears a shopkeeper in the Olympic Village who keeps a camera shop and sells Leicas missed two expensive models. Found it out when he cleaned up last night and by breakfast this morning they had both cameras—in the quarters of two of our boxers."

"Our boxers? Ours?" The Duke resented this. Also, he hardly believed it.

"Fact. Ask anyone who knows. What's more, they've been dismissed from the squad and are leaving tonight for Hamburg to sail for New York. Story we give out is that they're homesick. Homesick! But that's the way things are run over here."

So that was it. What you read in the newspapers wasn't always so. He'd heard that said many times, but here was evidence plainly before his eyes. The older man went on in an admiring voice.

"Yessir, they sure know how to do things here, and they know how to sell this sort of thing, believe me."

Helen, at the end of the line, who had said little, leaned over and broke in. "Yes, and they know how to sell Germany, too."

He looked up, surprised. Who was that good-looking, quiet-voiced girl? "Well, why not?"

"Oh, no reason, no reason, except I thought the idea of the Olympics was to sell sport, not any particular nation."

What would he say to that? He didn't say anything because further discussion was difficult as they approached the Stadium. Like thousands of bees round their hives, each seeking to enter his own swarm, the spectators rushed into the various gates. It seemed as if the whole of Berlin was out to watch this new sport, although it was not an especially good evening, blustery and chilly enough for an overcoat even though the month was August. Entering the Stadium this way was, he discovered, as impressive as marching out from underneath. From outside the structure was immense but not especially breathtaking, merely an enormous oval of about two stories divided in the middle by a balcony. It was only when you actually showed your card and walked inside that you realized its size. The whole thing was doubled with as much space hollowed below the ground as above, like a ship of which you only saw one half above the waterline. The huge hemisphere was nearly filled, and the Duke noticed opposite them a kind of breach in the structure which opened dramatically onto the *Reichssportfeld* beyond and gave a vista of dim blackness. Underneath this breach was the tunnel through which all the teams had marched onto the field on the opening afternoon.

"Takes your breath away, doesn't it?" said Helen, looking about the rapidly filling enclosure as they sat down.

"Yes." It did take your breath away. Somehow

it was more imposing up here looking down on the empty field below. Then Helen clutched suddenly at him.

The lights went out.

With their instinct for the dramatic, the authorities without any warning doused the Stadium in blackness for a second or two and then two huge and powerful searchlights spotted the two baseball nines coming onto the field from opposite ends of the ground. Their white uniforms glistened in the dazzling light as they marched up to the flagpole in center field and gave the Olympic salute. Then the lights went on again and soon the teams were spread out on the freshly lined diamond taking batting and fielding practice. All the while an announcer speaking German gave the spectators a description of baseball over the loudspeaker system.

"Something—well, almost terrifying about it. I mean the whole thing, and the people, their oneness, their unanimity. Isn't there?"

There was. Just what he'd felt without being able to express it. "Uhuh. That was what got me the other day when we marched in with those German boys and girls right behind us. Gosh, what a hand they gave them. Say, what's that he keeps saying, *Welt* . . . *Welt* . . . What is it?"

"*Weltmeister*. World's Champions. The team in the field. The World's Champions against the U.S. Olympics."

"You speak German?"

"A little. Were you in the Stadium by any chance yesterday morning? No, of course not, you all have to practice, don't you? I came over with Cecil Brocklehurst, he's a friend of my brother's who studied in England. . . ."

"You don't mean *the* Brocklehurst?"

"The same. Cecil George Vivian Brocklehurst. . . ."

"Vivian. I thought that was a girl's name. Vivian . . ."

"Don't make any cracks. It's a boy's name or a girl's name in England. I imagine you'll find he has the stuff in spite of his name. I told him about you and he's anxious to meet you. Yes, he is, too; he likes Americans and I think he's interested in the way we develop winners, though he won't admit it. Well, we wandered over here because there wasn't much doing, and guess what. The Stadium was filled. Absolutely. What do you think was going on? You'd never guess. Shot put. Trials."

"No!" He knew pretty well how exciting shot put trials were.

"Yes, sir. And at nine forty-five in the morning the whole place was jammed. I didn't stay much more than an hour because I had to report at the *Kuppelsalle*, that's the amphitheatre where they hold the fencing, but the crowd hung round till noon. And not a seat vacant."

"You mean they stayed here until noon for shot put trials? They must love sport. Or they must be nuts."

"Or else . . ."

"Or else what? What do you mean? I don't get you?" What was she trying to say? One had to watch this girl, she was always coming up with such strange ideas.

"Or else maybe they were told to show up."

"Told to come?"

"Certainly. By the government. I don't know, you understand, I'm just wondering. Doesn't seem to me you could get a hundred and ten thousand people out at nine forty in the morning to watch shot put trials unless there was some reason." Down below on the field there was a snappy double play, but although the announcer endeavored to explain it to the crowd and arouse their interest, they remained lethargic. In fact it was plain by the time the first few innings were over that the game was not taking very well with the Germans because here and there scattered individuals were leaving. Before long small gaps appeared in the stands.

"Ever hear of field handball?"

"Field handball? Where do they get these games from? I heard of field hockey for men today for the first time, and Slips says they have canoeing and gliding contests in these Olympics."

"I know. They've got some funny sports all right. This field handball is played outdoors with a large round ball by teams, that's all I know. Well, I met a fräulein yesterday who stopped outside the Stadium and asked me where the field hockey game was. Of course I didn't know there was such a game, and I asked her what it was like. She didn't know because she'd never seen one. So I said, 'Why do you go then?' What do you think she said? 'Because I have to use my card of admittance.' "

The Duke chuckled. It sounded true enough. By this time the sixth inning was coming up. Even by the lights which kept parts of the Stadium in shadow they could see that the structure was half empty and crowds were pouring toward the exits. "Looks like these folks don't enjoy our baseball. Oh, well, this game isn't so hot anyway. Tell me about Brocklehurst. Some people say he's the man who'll win the event. Sanderson doesn't think so. Wonder how he trains; do you know?"

"No, not much. I really don't know him well. I met him several years ago in the States. All I can discover about his training is that it doesn't make much sense to an American. He probably knows what's best."

"In what way?"

"I mean in preparing for these games. He did most of his work last winter, he told me, and hasn't done much of anything the past six weeks. During the fall and winter he ran every distance from the half to three miles. Maybe that's because he has to run your event and also a relay race of some kind."

"Yes, I believe he's in their 1,600 meter relay team. What does he do now?"

"Now? Oh, anything at all. He just trains any old way. This morning he went swimming."

"Swimming!" The Duke was shocked. Swimming! Slips Ellis would as soon have told him to jump off the tower of the Stadium as go swimming the week of the race. "Does his coach know it?"

"I guess so. Anyway, he pretty well runs his

own show. He's experienced, you know. But he went swimming and this afternoon he's practicing starts and jogging for a couple of miles and then going for a walk. Says the one thing he's afraid of is staleness. Thinks most of our runners are overtrained."

"You know, that's funny. I was watching Lou Schumacher at breakfast this morning; he seemed white and drawn, sort of. Shouldn't be surprised if there was something in that idea. Of course it's different for different runners; now me, I need work to get back where I was last spring. Say . . . look at that hit. . . ." A player smacked a triple to center field and there were some feeble cheers from the deserted stands. The Stadium by this time was nearly empty. The announcer tried hard to pump up interest through the tone in his voice, but with little success. Then suddenly he changed his pitch. *"Achtung. Achtung."*

"Wait a minute." She listened to the announcer's words. As he finished his sentence the entrances began filling up. "Hear that? There's going to be a military band concert immediately after the ball game."

"Watch those babies come back again." It had taken some time to empty the Stadium, but as soon as the announcer finished the crowd started to return, and when the last man was out in the ninth, the big enclosure was filled with Germans to whom a military band concert was one thing and a baseball game something else again.

The next afternoon was fixed for the Duke's time trial. That would give him four or five days to rest before the race itself. Slips was pleased with his work and he himself felt progress, saw progress daily. Best of all he felt like running. Once more running was fun. So after a brisk workout and limbering-up exercises in the morning, he made ready after lunch for the time trial on the practice track outside the Stadium. Sam Honeyman, who had nosed him out of second place in the Olympic tryouts at home, was to pace him for the last six hundred yards. He was faster than he had been the month before, that much he was certain of. Dressing carefully, he went down to the track in what was almost the first sunshine since the games had started, and began warming up. After some bending and dipping, he stepped on the track and jogged slowly up and down the straightaway. It was a fast track, well made, and he liked it. A tow-headed runner, in the white German sweater with the black eagle on it, stood watching him. When the Duke paused and hesitated beside the track, this German came up and standing stiffly with his legs together, bowed over and said:

"Pleez. . . ."

He mentioned something, probably his name, but the Duke didn't understand. He did understand the extended hand and took it. A long, lean, firm hand it was, too. In spite of their ceremonial manners you couldn't help liking these people, so clean-cut, so good-looking, so trim and, above all, so friendly. With an appealing smile and an awkward English accent the stranger began to ask questions. What did he do those exercises for? Always before racing, so? How long had he run? So?

"Look here; if you really want to know anything about distance running you ought to ask Lou Schumacher standing over there. You know, Schumacher, he was 1,500 meter champion in the last Olympics. . . ."

But the German was unimpressed. "Yah, yah, I like you, I like your style, pleez. . . ."

That frank, pleasant, and open face, that shock of tow hair across the forehead. Now where had he seen this man before? Of course, in the newsreels. It was Von Gerhardt.

"Why, say, aren't you Von Gerhardt?"

"Yah, yah, Von Gerhardt." He pronounced the first word of his name as if it were spelled "Fon."

"But look here, you shouldn't be asking me questions about running. I barely got on this team. Just barely—with a third place in the try-outs, understand? *Verstehe.* . . ."

"*Yah, Ich verstehe.*" He nodded his head and smiled.

"But you shouldn't be asking me questions." This was ridiculous. The great Von Gerhardt, the best middle distance runner in Europe, questioning a newcomer to the American team who had only got on by a fluke. The Duke suddenly became self-conscious and hoped no one noticed them. Must ask him some questions. Unfortunately he couldn't think of anything to ask. "What do you do?" he blurted out in desperation.

"Pleez?"

"I say what's your business? What do you do?"

"Who? Me? I run." He rolled the r's in the last word. It sounded like rrrrun.

"Yes, but I mean when you don't. You don't run all the time."

"Yah." He nodded his head vigorously. "I run."

"You mean you're a . . . a professional?"

"*Ach, nein. . . .*"

"Well, then, I don't understand. Who pays you, I mean how do you live?"

"The Reich. I mus' run for the Reich, yah?" He was eloquent about it. "Since last Olympics, I come fourth, I train, I work for deses Olympics, yah?"

"You mean since the last Olympic Games you've been living off the state and training just for these Games here in Berlin? But what do you use for money?"

"*Nein*, no money."

"Just your living."

"Yah." There was something which staggered the Duke about the German's calm acceptance that his life belonged to the government and that if he was a good runner he should put himself at their disposal to be developed and trained as a champion for three or four long years. How did these people ever get started in business or a profession? He wanted to know more, but Slips was calling. The German in his running trousers drew his legs together, bent over stiffly and held out his hand. The Duke took it; not the last time he was to shake hands with Friedrich Von Gerhardt.

Whatever else the German was, he wasn't dumb. As the Duke nervously toed the line, waiting for Slips to give him the word, the blond Teuton stood there quietly watching. Of those next agonizing minutes the Duke didn't recall much later except Gerhardt's face flashing past him as he rounded into the straightaway, looking, measuring him, taking in his weak points as he caught the pacer up ahead. Then the concentration and the pain forced everything from his mind as he made an effort to hold on grimly in those last death struggles of the race, as he tried to catch Sam's flying feet, caught him finally, was even, was beating him, fell back ever so slightly, and finished at his shoulder in a spasm of agony, falling in a heap on the grass beside the track.

Slips ran across, picked him up, and tried to walk him round, but he could hardly stand at first. Finally, with the arm of the coach supporting him, he was lugged and carried across to the dressing room.

There, stretched out on a bench in the warm interior, his breath slowly returned. "How . . . how was it, Slips?"

"All right, boy. All right. You just lie there."

The Duke was still in too much pain to question the coach further, and after the shower and rub-down Slips had gone. The time was good or it was bad. Good, he hoped, and felt. Only he wished Gerhardt hadn't been there watching so closely.

Slips, leaving the locker rooms, met Helen coming back to the women's quarters for supper.

"Just given our boy a time trial. He's in there now dressing."

"How'd he do? Was it good? Oh, I hope it was good, Slips?"

Slips said nothing. He merely raised his eyebrows expressively and put both hands palms down to the ground. Then he hurried along. She stood wondering. An expressive gesture, but just what did it mean?

14

His voice, clear and sharp, went across Germany, across a wide sea, across the British Isles, across an ocean, across two thousand miles of land and into the living room of that home in Waterloo, Iowa.

". . . making an Olympic record and a world's record of twenty-six feet, six and five-eight inches, and in the last jump, folks, that colored boy almost jumped clean out of Germany." He paused, chuckling at his witticism.

"And now in the next event we have . . ." The telephone jangled from another world, bringing them both to their feet. "Just someone telling us his heat is coming up. Your Aunt Kate, most probably. She hasn't turned her radio off day and night all week. What'll that be; the fourth or fifth today? I'm going to take the receiver off the hook, Mother. Yes, I am. Can't have that thing breaking into the middle of the race. Remember, if he doesn't finish one, two, or three today this will be his only race over there." Mr. Wellington walked across the room and removed the receiver. The jangling changed to a gurgle, died away, and once more that voice coming across an ocean filled the room.

". . . so now, folks, we come to one of the more important races, the first heat of the 1,500 meter run. There'll be four heats this afternoon and then the finals Friday afternoon with the men who win first, second, or third places qualifying." How easy when you say it like that, thought the father, picturing the Duke, white and nervous, stepping to the starting line in Berlin. How easy when you say it fast like that, and how little anyone really knew about it. "We have three representatives, Lou Schumacher, who won the event in the last Olympics—he's going very well over here; Sam Honeyman, the star distance man of the New York A.C., and then, and then . . ." For a moment he forgot the other name. Mr. Wellington glanced across at his wife and smiled with the corner of his mouth drawn up. ". . . and then, yes, of course, and then Jimmy Wellington of Harvard. Lou Schumacher is drawn in the third heat with Marcel Dupont of France and Fritz Neckermann of Germany. In the second heat is Brocklehurst, C. G. V. Brocklehurst, the sensational Englishman who's been breaking all records in Australia this past winter. In the third heat Sam Honeyman, bracketed with Davison of Australia and Carp of Switzerland. In the final heat Friedrich Von Gerhardt, the German star. Over here they expect great things from him in this race. In the first heat Wellington of the United States is running second from the pole, next to him Hans Ostermark of Sweden, next Luigi Mariano of Italy . . ."

His voice disappeared as Spot, the Airedale, rose off the rug barking.

"SHUT UP, SPOT. SHUT UP. Keep quiet. Oh . . . it's the laundry man. Go out, boy, go on." He went to the door, dragging the reluctant

Spot by the collar, throwing him out and taking the package with one movement. The door shut. Save for some yawps from outside, silence descended.

". . . and . . . and last, and finally, in the middle lane nearest the Stadium, John F. K. Handley of Canada. That's twelve men in all, twelve good men in this heat and one American, Jimmy Wellington. We hope to place two men in the finals; 'course the class comes in the second and third heats with Schumacher and Brocklehurst and Gerhardt . . . no, correction . . . Gerhardt is in the third heat with Honeyman. Now they're getting ready. Remember the distance, 1,500 meters, that's a little under one mile which would be . . . well, exactly 1,609 meters, and it's about but not quite four times round the track. This track here in Berlin measures four hundred meters in circumference, so four times round would be nearly a mile. Now they're ready. The starter's going back. Wellington second from the pole between Ostermark of Sweden and Soulier of France, Mariano of Italy, I should say, and then Soulier . . . there goes the starter, his gun is raised. . . ."

"BANG." The shot sounded as if it had gone off in the room.

"They're off . . . Ostermark . . . Mariano . . . Ertzberger, Germany . . . Soulier . . . Handley . . . *and* Wellington in the rear, almost last, they got the jump on him . . . it seemed . . . he's back in there now with . . . with Kress of Greece . . . Ostermark takes the turn . . . Mariano just at his heels . . . then Ungavary of Hungary . . . Soulier . . . Ertzberger . . . Handley . . . Kress . . . Wellington pretty well back . . . he got jostled badly in that first fight . . . now coming into the second turn, no change . . . Ostermark and Mariano still fighting it out . . . and opening up a gap . . . there goes Wellington past Kress . . . he's out after Ertzberger . . . he's nailed him . . . he's running well . . . now he seems to be after Ungavary in earnest . . . he's still in there trying, this boy. . . ."

"What's the man think?" interrupted Mr. Wellington indignantly.

"Shss. . . ."

". . . so into the second turn . . . Ostermark . . . Mariano . . . in front now going up the backstretch . . . then Handley of Canada running extremely well . . . hullo, there goes Wellington . . . he's after Soulier . . . he's right on his heels . . . he's got him, I think . . .

no . . . yes . . . he's carrying the Frenchman along with him and they both seem to be gaining on Handley. Say, this may be a battle after all. Only thing, Ostermark and Mariano have such a lead, a pretty big lead and it's the end of the second lap. With the field this way. Ostermark . . . Mariano . . . ten, no twelve or fifteen yards, then Handley, Soulier and Wellington bunched, Ungavary, Ertzberger, Georges and Kress and the others out of it. Round the turn, Ostermark and Mariano nose and nose . . . the Italian going ahead slightly . . . no, Ostermark cleverly keeps the pole and edges him off . . . a beautiful race, oh, a beautiful race . . . they go down the stretch together, almost together . . . SAY, LOOK AT THAT . . . here comes Wellington with Soulier right on his heels and what a drive those boys have . . . they're after Handley sure thing now, no mistake about it . . . the three of them go round the turn . . . the pace is faster . . . Handley only a little in front . . . into the stretch . . . they're stepping out for the leaders. . . ."

"CLANG-CLANG-CLANG-CLANG." The strident bell went through Mrs. Wellington's heart.

". . . and the last lap of all, the bell for

the last lap . . . and are they fighting it . . . going out in this order . . . Ostermark . . . Mariano . . . Handley . . . Wellington and Soulier bunched . . . fifteen yards . . . Ungavary . . . back of him Ertzberger and Georges . . . what a race this is . . . about ten yards separates the two leaders from the next three men, but now they've taken the turn . . . they're gaining, yes, the men behind are closing up . . . no doubt about it . . . there they go . . . Mariano . . . Ostermark . . . Handley . . . Wellington . . . Soulier . . . Handley moving up now . . . Handley in second place and chasing the Italian . . . Wellington going up . . . Handley in the lead, Handley first, Mariano . . . Wellington . . . Ostermark . . . Soulier, there he goes, there goes Wellington . . . Wellington by a yard . . . Wellington by two yards . . . Wellington by three, by four yards . . . Wellington wins, Handley second, Soulier third, Mariano fourth, Ostermark, Sweden, fifth, and Ungavary, sixth. . . ."

Up in the press box fourteen hundred and eighteen sportswriters from lands as far apart as Turkey and Trinidad gasped and turned to each other. Wellington? The name resounded up and down the benches in different tones and with different accents. Who was he? An unknown. Ah, these Americans. They were like that, always up to some trick. One could never trust them. Ah, they were clever, these Americans. Not Schumacher, everyone knew Schumacher, not even Honeyman who had run several years before, but a stranger, a newcomer. They had kept him hidden, said nothing about him to anyone. Wellington. The time went up on the big board beside the Duke's name. The time was not fast and not slow, either. Meanwhile the press questioned each other about this new figure. Only Jim Casey and a few of the sportswriters from the eastern papers had ever heard of Wellington. The Duke. Certainly. Duke Wellington. You remember. Harvard track captain; Slips Ellis brought him along, you know.

"Oh, yes, that Harvard flash-in-the-pan. Don't you remember, Bill? He made a world's record in the two mile last year and then petered out completely. Hasn't done anything since. Did he win the mile in the Intercollegiates, Henry, this last spring? Did he? He must have . . ."

"Duke Wellington. Sure, I know him." As usual Casey knew everyone. They crowded about him for information regarding this unknown third-stringer who had made the headlines with a victory in his heat in the 1,500 meters. "We ought to have three men in the finals then. Will this bird make trouble for Schumacher? Or Gerhardt? *Or* Brocklehurst? Time good, but nothing amazing. No one really first class in his heat. But say, did you notice he let himself get jammed behind the field at the start. A lousy start. What'll he do Friday if he gets a good start, hey?"

As the Duke told Slips the next evening he wasn't worrying about the finals. "You know, almost for the first time since I started running I'm not bothered about this race. I've done better than I hoped, better than anyone hoped and reached the finals. I'm set. Somehow now there doesn't seem to be the responsibility there usually is. I don't feel anything hanging on it like there was at Cambridge. I'd like to do well, but I'm not anxious."

"That's great, boy. I'm tickled you feel like that. Just the way I want for you to feel. Get a good sleep and forget tomorrow."

"You know, Slips, I'd like to do well for you. Know that, don't you? And if I hope to land a job in some school teaching track I suppose it would be fine if I could place. But I'm not counting . . ."

"You'll place well. You'll win."

He spoke quietly but firmly. The Duke could see he meant it.

"Win? With Brocklehurst and Schumacher and . . ."

"You'll win. You'll win if you run the right sort of race. Even old Sanderson is sure you'll be up there. Never even knew you were on the team until you ran that heat yesterday; now he's all steamed up about your chances. He isn't saying this, but he agrees with me that Schumacher is through."

"Through! Lou Schumacher through! Schumacher finished!"

"Finished. Absolutely. Washed out. Why not? He's been running steadily winter and summer since the last Olympics, trying to clean up. Last winter he made over twenty-five hundred. . . ."

Stories, vague rumors, jokes tossed about in the dressing room, guesses and reports now crystallized. Slips knew. Slips never speculated. Slips didn't say things he wasn't sure about. "Schumacher takes money; that what you mean?"

"Duke, you know a man isn't running in the University of Illinois relays one night and then flying to Los Angeles to run in the Coliseum the next night, and taking a plane to beat you in the

Studebaker Mile two nights later in New York, without something more than just expenses. He's been well taken care of financially, physically he's used himself up. The man you want to watch is Brocklehurst."

"Well, what about Gerhardt?"

"I'm much more worried about the Englishman. Tell you why. Gerhardt is coming. He's learning all the time and going to be good. But Brocklehurst is at his peak right now. He's one sweet runner, that baby, and there's only one way to beat him; be sure and get command of the race yourself."

The Duke hated to hear him say this. "Run a front race? That what you mean, Slips?"

"Yes. Well, no, not necessarily. Depends. I don't necessarily mean running a front race, although you may have to. This man Brocklehurst like Lou and every first-class star is a great showman. I suppose there's a bit of the showman in every good athlete in every sport. Think that's your main trouble, Duke, you aren't enough of a showman . . . oh, I admit, it's a good fault. But now you take Brocklehurst; if you boys let him run his own race, he'll win. You mustn't allow it. See what I'm driving at?"

"Yes, but how? What should I do?"

"I'm telling you. His whole ability is predicated on running a front race, or, let me put it this way, running his own race, as I said. Understand? He wants to be boss, to be in command, to run his own show his own way. Like a championship tennis player imposing his personality on an opponent, haven't you ever seen that? You have? Sure, of course. Same thing with Brocklehurst. To beat this Englishman takes more than guts, more than race ability, it takes tactics: intelligence, cunning, shrewdness. You've gotta bother him all the way. Gotta harry him. Get me?"

"Yes, but, Slips, that isn't . . ."

"I know. I knew you'd bring that up. Isn't the kind of a race you like, you're used to. You enjoy that sprint at the end; you have a sprint and you like to use it. You'll need it on the last lap when the Britisher turns on the heat, believe me. You should have seen him burn up those last four hundred yards in his heat; it was great running. Sometimes I think you are always slow getting away half on purpose, that you really get a kick out of being last and working up bit by bit through the field."

"Yeah, maybe I do at that."

"Thought so. You haven't changed much, Duke, since the old days at Cambridge. Look here, you trust me, don't you?"

"Of course, Slips."

"All right. Forget your usual methods. Run a different race tomorrow. You see, the field is so good you can't run the kind of a race you'd like; you must run the kind of race to beat men like Gerhardt and Brocklehurst."

"And Schumacher."

"Forget Schumacher, will you? Forget him. Even if he gets a ten yard lead, forget him. He'll be trying to do to Brocklehurst just what you are trying to do, that's where you both have an advantage. But never mind him, concentrate on this Englishman. You gotta get out there in front and get there at the start."

"Yes, but . . ."

"No buts. I'm telling you how to win. You can win if you chuck away your old tactics; get in front or as near as you can and stay right there with Brocklehurst. Don't let him move away from you. Bother him. Harry him. Make him change his pace. That'll upset his plans, and he has his ideas how to run this race. It's like that football game last fall; Harvard had her attack all planned and Yale upset it by a sliding defense, remember? He's going to be awfully worried by tactics of that sort, especially coming from you. Lou he knows all about and he isn't worried—that is he won't be bothered much by anything Lou does. He knows all about Lou. Gerhardt, maybe, yes, he thinks he can handle the German. But if he ever gets a look at your back it won't make him comfortable."

That's what the Duke went to bed upon. There was no conversation between the two roommates as the lights went out. They lay thinking. Finally he heard Harry's gentle snore. Harry wasn't running the next afternoon.

As soon as it was light he rose and looked out. Cloudy with a drizzle. Not so good. He tossed in bed, lay there until eight, had breakfast and a massage in the morning. Then a short walk, lunch, and he began to get ready for the race. Telegrams started early and kept coming; from his family, from Fog now working on a magazine in New York, from Mickey in the West, from classmates in college. There was a note wishing him good luck from Helen Davis, and when he returned from lunch to his room half a dozen more wires were waiting. It was almost like Christmas. Slips was there, keeping out one or two energetic reporters who wanted to talk to him, learn his background and something about his personality, "just in case," as one of them expressed it afterward to the coach.

"No good, boys, you can see him all you like after it's over. Nothing doing now."

At two they walked over to the dressing rooms. By this time he was considerably more nervous than he had been before the heat, although he noticed that there wasn't the terror the races in college always caused. With Slips' help he undressed and dressed again.

"Raining outside?" he asked one of the pole vaulters coming in.

"Naw. Stopped. But cold; stinking weather." The whole week had been gloomy, chilly, and unpleasant. He put on his sweat clothes and with Slips went out back of the *Reichssportfeld* to the practice track and started his workout. To the few German spectators he seemed demented. First he started walking back and forth over a space of twenty yards, slowly then faster and faster and faster, until he was like a man pacing the floor with jitters. He kept this up for twenty minutes, and then paused at Slips' command.

After a short rest he began jogging slowly

round the track, stretching his legs forward and backward. Occasionally he stopped for his exercises, which consisted in leaning over and touching the track with the palms of his hands without bending either knee. Every few hundred yards he repeated this. He tossed his head like a thoroughbred horse, snorting loudly to clear his nostrils. From the other side of the track he saw Lou Schumacher appear with old Sanderson and begin his warming-up. He snorted some more. Breathing was a vital part of running. Then he began to take a turn round the track, gradually increasing his speed and making a couple of circuits of the track at a fast sprinting speed. A whistle from Slips across the field stopped him. He slowed down and jogged over.

"All right, boy, rest a minute or two. Now take off your sweat clothes." From the lockers came a long, tall, loose-jointed blond man with enormously long legs. He stepped onto the track, kicking his legs before him and prancing like a horse. The Duke's first sight of the great Brocklehurst.

They walked over to the competitor's entrance together. There was a sign up of the next event.

"1,500 METER LAUF." The 1,500 meters run. The Duke paused and turned.

"Good-bye, Slips. If I don't do all right, it won't be your fault."

"Fine, boy. I'm not worrying. Good luck, keep your head, that's all."

Now he was inside the Stadium. That tremendous double-decked structure was jammed. From below it was enormous; yes, it was impressive standing there and looking up at the sea of faces, row upon row, until you could only distinguish a vague blur. Except Hitler in his box, in that same brown costume, surrounded by the same officers in uniform. The Duke stepped onto the track, a beautiful track, firm, hard, and springy, and trotted round to the starting line. From far across the field a sharp chorus cut the air.

"RAY, RAY, RAY, U.S.A., RAY, RAY, RAY, U.S.A., U.S.A., WELLINGTON, WELLINGTON, WELLINGTON."

A rooting section from home. He waved his hand in their direction and they yelled back their support. It was almost like the Stadium at Cambridge, save for the queer, unfamiliar-looking people in the stands close down to the track. Then a shrill shriek rose. He looked across to see Brocklehurst stepping onto the cinders. Several hundred English boy scouts were cheering.

"We Want YOU to Win. We Want YOU to Win. We Want YOU to Win. . . ."

He moved slowly along toward the starting line. The starter, a big burly German in a white suit, shook hands with him in a brisk and businesslike but not unfriendly fashion. The Clerk of the Course with his board in his hand came over and looked at his number, checking it against the list on his board. "Vellington, yah?" The Duke nodded. Lou Schumacher at one side was peeling down to his track suit. They shook hands.

"Best o' luck, Wellington."

"To you, Lou. I'll be right behind you." The older man shook his head and held out his hand. The Duke noticed it was icy cold. Queer, he thought, for an experienced runner like that. Another hand was extended. Von Gerhardt, clicking his heels as usual, even in his track suit. Then Brocklehurst came over; tall, long legs, with a nice smile and upper teeth that stuck out prominently. He seemed more of a real athlete and less tense than anyone.

"How are you?" They clasped hands and then he shook hands with Lou, Von Gerhardt, and Dupont the Frenchman.

Now the starter was arranging them. Dupont

on the pole, Handley of Canada next, and . . .
no . . . yes, he was motioning to the Duke. The
Duke was next, just where he'd been in his heat,
second from the pole. Well, you couldn't ask for
anything better than that. He pinned one corner
of his number firmly on his chest again, and dug
his holes in the beautifully packed cinders. A
wonderful track all right. Lou was two down the
line. He grinned, but his grin was forced. The
Duke saw with relief that Brocklehurst was almost on the outside which meant more distance
to cover to reach the pole by the first turn. The
starter was saying something in German and then
repeated it in English, but the Duke was too
tense to catch what he was saying.

Then a brisk command.

"Auf den Marken. Fertig. . . ."

"Ah . . ." The gasp went up all over the Stadium as Dupont slipped away, burst down the
track, jogged to a standstill and returned. The
starter's words again were beyond the Duke's
comprehension, and the Frenchman, tall, slim,
nervous, came back shaking his head and expostulating. Now they were bent over once more.

"Auf den Marken. Ferrrrtig. . . ."

He was ahead. No, Dupont next to him was

first, but he was close beside him in the stretch. Fast, fast as the devil, a regular 220 pace into the turn. This time someone else was taking the licking on the first corner, one of the wolves behind. Coming into the stretch there was a head at his shoulder, and inch by inch a figure surged forward. The Duke moved out to pass Dupont, went up slowly, but that figure beside him stuck. Brocklehurst. How he must have run those few hundred yards to come up from outside and swing ahead!

As they swept together past the Frenchman the stands were rising, yelling and shrieking. God, what a pace, what speed, he'd last a lap, two laps maybe, that's all. Just let me stick it two laps. Two laps is all I ask. Already it was hard to breathe, and he could hear the labored snorts from the Englishman at his side. Try as he would he couldn't shake him, and slowly Brocklehurst pulled ahead and took the turn. Immediately the pace slackened.

The Duke remembered. Through the haze of fatigue coming over him he remembered. Now then. Moving into the straightaway he edged over and cut loose with everything he had. It caught the other man by surprise, and he passed the stands with the cheers from the American contingent in his ears.

"U.S.A., U.S.A., RAY, RAY, U.S.A."

Then the sound vanished from his consciousness as he took the turn and felt that pounding on his heels. What a pace; how could the man stand it? But the man could. The man did. He came on with a burst of energy that was inhuman, and again went into the lead. While all the time the wolves behind were at the Duke's heels; pound-pound, sluff-sluff, pound-pound.

Surely someone would crack. As they rounded the turn, with Brocklehurst two yards ahead, he glanced back and saw the field well strung out behind. But there were men close up to him, and there was that devil just ahead. He disliked him, suddenly he felt a hatred for the fellow. The man wasn't human. Now, they were in the stretch once more, but no use trying to jump him, he'd expect it here. Indeed all the Duke could do was keep within range of the flying cinders from the other's spikes. They pricked his bare ankles, and although his whole frame was aching, those cinders irritated him most of all. The man wasn't human. Not human. How could he keep such a pace?

He couldn't. He slowed down, not much but enough as they rounded the turn for the Duke with a desperate effort to move up before they hit the straightaway and work up even. If only he could get past; he shut his eyes, opened them, thought, tried not to think, and then suddenly was moving past. He caught the pole with a feeling of joy. If he flivvered now it wouldn't be because he hadn't carried out Slips' instructions. He was through, he was done, he was finished, he was beaten. But he was in front.

In front at last. There he comes, there he comes. The wolf was there, beside him, waiting to strike. The Duke somehow managed to open up his stride, went ahead a little, and took the next turn in the lead. For the first time confidence came to him through the envelope of weariness that surrounded him. If Brocklehurst didn't pass now it meant the pace had told. There was a chance.

The finish line flashed past. Third lap. Hold him off, hold him off, hold . . . no fun this . . . running front man . . . never again, no, never again, never run again, Slips, never . . . there he comes. The heavy breathing appeared at his right shoulder, at his right elbow, by his right side as they fought for that lead. Neck and neck they rounded the turn; elbows swinging in unison, they beat into the stretch together.

Worry him. Worry, said Slips, worry, worry him . . . make him do the trying . . . but the Duke was dead. All he wanted to do was stop, cease the torture. They'd taken the next turn almost before he realized it, and then dimly it came to him that the Stadium was on its feet, frenzied with excitement and noise. All he really knew through that fog of fatigue was the powerful frame beside him, unshakable, dauntless, mouth open like his own, urging on. No, Slips, not again, not again, Slips, just this once, but never again, never. . . .

Something pounded at him from a remote distance. The gun! The gun for the bell lap. The sound struck that agonized man at his side, slapped him like a whip, sent him forward, an inch, a foot, almost enough to move over to the precious pole. When something happened.

He went back. Slowly, not much at first. Imperceptibly. They were even. Now he was going back, enabling the Duke to take the lead unchallenged. Only four hundred, three hundred yards, and the man was going back. His figure was slipping away just as consciousness seemed to be slipping away from the Duke, whose body was all pain and torture. No, Slips, not this again, not this . . . still he was ahead . . . the man was going back . . . going back to Nassau's Halls . . . going back . . . he was ahead. He was in front. Brocklehurst was going back. He lost the pound-pound of that rhythmical step as the last turn came up. Another sound, another step came from the rear. Wolves. He could see nothing but he knew the finish was close now . . . just a last final plunge . . . everything . . .give everything . . . now . . . fight it off . . . that wolf . . . wolves . . . ahead the string . . . there . . . the string . . . it snapped across his chest . . .

15

He was in almost the only place in the whole of Berlin and certainly the only place in the *Reichssportfeld* where he could be unmolested. That was hidden away beside Helen Davis in the crowd in the Stadium.

Two days previously he was an unknown. Merely a Harvard senior who had managed to get a third in the 1,500 meter Olympic tryouts in New York. That boy who was always around with Slips Ellis, the assistant track coach. Then the race, and in a little under four minutes he changed into a world celebrity. Before he actually returned to his little room in the Olympic Village, just a room in one bungalow exactly like every other room in the other hundred and fifty bungalows, the cables were waiting. They continued to pour in all that night. Cables of love and delight from the family at home, from his friends and relatives in the States, from the principal of the high school in Waterloo, from the Chamber of Commerce. There were also other cables from unknown persons, names he'd never heard of before. Someone who wished to act as his manager to make a professional tour; someone else who wanted to be his radio agent; from a man in Los Angeles who asked whether he was interested in the movies as a career and offered to sign a contract with him. There were requests of all sorts: for articles from big weekly magazines at home, for his presence as speaker at the banquets of sporting associations, suggestions that he endorse all sorts of things as dissimilar as candy sticks, models of new automobiles, and clothing of every description. "Will you try get home for sports day State Fair Iowa proud her son sincere congratulations wonderful victory?" "Would you care appear Rudy Vallee Hour directly following return New York with best wishes please advise?" "Will you help cause amateur sport run in kay of see open meet eighteenth next month wire collect all best wishes congratulations great victory?" "Hope can manage speak our annual banquet sixteenth fee two hundred congratulations splendid victory america proud stop advise."

All that night and the next day and the next. Sitting under that deluge of telegrams was bad, but it was worse reading them. There was nothing to do but sign for them, open them, read them, and chuck them away. Meanwhile a spring flood of reporters, sportswriters, and radio commentators poured into the little room, questioning him, taking notes of everything he said, while he stood eyeing them and wondering what on earth he had said that was worth printing. They listened to his replies with a respect and deference that surprised and annoyed him.

"Honest, Helen, you'd think I was someone important. Really important, I mean, not an Olympic winner. Older men, too. They sit round with their mouths open as if I was a teacher and they were pupils. It's sickening. And the questions. The same old questions; everyone has the same line. Where did I learn to run? How did I learn to run? Is it true Slips Ellis developed me? What did it seem like to shake hands with Hitler? What was my greatest thrill? 'Thrill,' seems to be a pet word of the radio men. If I hear that word 'thrill' again— Last night I told one chap there wasn't any thrill to it, just plain hell all the way, every meter. And he said, 'Oh,' like that, and looked at me as if I'd been nuts. Wish he'd been out there on the firing line instead of sitting up in the press box looking for a thrill. Thrill . . . huh. . . ."

"The autograph fiends would be harder for me to take. When we came in just now I thought you'd never get away, never."

"That's boys and girls, mostly. I like 'em. They're awful cunning, those towheads. But the grown-ups sitting round gaping at you, asking idiotic questions. All leading up to the same thing of course. . . ."

"You mean they want to know when you'll turn professional?"

"Yes. And they can't figure out I'm telling the truth when I say I won't."

"That's because all the other men who won

are turning. I understand the colored boys have already announced the dates they become professionals."

"Let them. I like to run and maybe I'll want to run again later on, after I get a rest and get away from all this. Now I'm sick and tired of it, but in a couple of months probably running will be fun once more. Casey is about the only one who understands my point of view. 'But you could clean up,' they all say. 'But I don't want to clean up,' I say. Then they look at me."

"Casey's smart. He knew what you'd do, knew every move you'd make before you made it."

"Maybe. The others didn't. Don't anyway. Here's another funny angle. They had Brocklehurst and Dupont and Schumacher in every pose and posture you can imagine, and just about every costume, too. Why, Brocklehurst, they must have had a couple of hundred snaps of that boy, they've been taking him at practice every day. But they just didn't think to get me at all, so after the meet those camera men like to mob me. Friday I was the friend of Slips Ellis, the track coach who was chucked out of Harvard, and yesterday I couldn't step from the door without the cameras clicking like castanets. Prom-

ised I'd show up for them in track clothes, so
this morning we spent a couple of hours re-
running that race. Must have been fifty photographers there. Say, what's that mean—that thing
on the scoreboard now?"

"*Hochsprung*. High jump. In German *Kugel-
stof* is shot put and *Hurden lauf* is hurdles. Look
at those girls run."

A woman's relay race was in progress with
the home team well in the lead. The Stadium
was in a delirium of joy as their girls sped round
the turn for the last exchange of the baton, certain winners, when there was a mix-up, a bob-
ble, and the stick rolled on the ground. The
American girls in second place went ahead to
win easily while the crowd groaned in despair
and the big scoreboard showed the names of the
winners in the order of their finish.

U.S.A.

GROSS BRITANIEN

SCHWEIZ

HOLLAND

DEUTSCHLAND

"Look, Duke, look at that poor girl." She
pointed down to the grass beside the finish line

where, with the race over, the girl who had dropped the baton was walking along, crying bitterly, her head in her hands, shoulders shaking. A teammate beside her with one arm round her waist attempted to console her, but the other was racked with sobs until she finally disappeared under the Stadium.

There was a silence over the crowd. "That baby is certainly in wrong," he remarked.

"Yes, she takes it hard. But they all do." The Stadium sat quietly with little or no applause as the winning American team came out to be crowned with the wreaths of olive. It was an ominous quiet. Then two minutes later a roar broke out and the huge packed structure once again became frenzied with happiness. The *Hochsprung*. A German victory, the first in this event in the Olympic Games. Simultaneously the crowd burst into song. Arms outstretched they rose, a hundred thousand persons, singing their national anthem in unison at the top of their lungs. *Deutschland Über Alles*.

"Sing like they meant it," he shouted in her ear.

She nodded.

"They do." Then, the song over, the whole Stadium broke into the song of the party, the

Horst Wessel hymn, while the big black and gold swastika rose to the flagpole. They roared, a kind of yell that had defiance in it, a shout of victory, a shout both exultant and provocative. The foreigners in their section reserved for athletes looked about uneasily, and the Duke realized that there were aspects of this stern, strong nation which were less attractive as one knew them better. All at once the Games and the military regime surrounding them became acutely distasteful.

"Helen, I'd kind of enjoy getting away from all this."

"Where can we go? If we leave before the gang those autograph hounds will follow you up to your doorstep."

"No, not leave the Stadium. I mean get away from the Games, from Berlin, from Germany. I've had enough. Understand?"

"Yes, I do. Because I've had plenty for a week. I thought it was just because I was disappointed at losing; you know how it is, and I'm glad you have the same attitude. The intenseness of those German girl fencers and their anguish when they were beaten was awful. I didn't enjoy it one little bit. This whole show was great at first, it was organized beautifully and fairly run, impressive and all that. But now these people seem to be losing all control. Listen. Duke, why don't you come along down to Paris with me tomorrow? Mother and sister are landing from Le Havre with the car and we plan to tour Provence. You'd like it. Be great if you could come along."

"A good idea! I'm all through here. No reason I know of why I can't. Sure I'd like to. Father gave me some cash to travel through Europe after the Games and it would be much more fun with you people. Slips has to go somewhere with some team in a dual meet of some kind, and Harry Painton's family are taking him on a cruise with them. Leave here tomorrow, do you? That's quick work, but it suits me fine; the quicker the better. In that case I'll get back and start cleaning things up. Lucky my release from the team has been all approved and that's one bit of red tape out of the way. Let's go."

The small room in their bungalow was filled and overfilled that evening. Before the race, Slips and one or two of the boys in adjoining rooms were the only people they saw; now it was seldom empty. All sorts and conditions of men found reasons why they had to see the Duke. Officials he had never met, men who hadn't bothered to speak to him aboard ship, radio announcers he had never seen before and didn't care to see again, sportswriters who called him "Duke" affectionately but whose names he couldn't remember, all made themselves at home on Harry's up-ended bags, on the two beds, on the small chairs, and even on the unoccupied parts of the floor. With Harry's help he tried to pack, his lungs smarting in the smoke-laden atmosphere. In between packing, signing for telegrams, and answering questions he listened to the conversation and especially to the remarks of Casey seated in a corner chewing on his pipe.

"Boy, if I hafta stand up for this here now Dutch song—those two songs I mean, if I have to keep hopping up for them much more, something's gonna burst. Hear what Mike Dolan, the swing band leader, did? Seems Ernest Brewer's little girl was next to him the other afternoon when the Germans were winning, and they had to keep rising for those hymns. Next day she found out who Mike was and asked him for his autograph. He wrote on her program: 'To Betty Brewer, my lifelong companion during the singing of the *Horst Wessel* song in the Berlin Olympics.' "

A telegraph boy knocked and came in.

"*Bitte* . . ." Harry Painton mechanically took the handful of envelopes, signed for them, and placed them on a pile of unopened despatches on the little table.

"Yeah, that's about it. Say, Duke, no fooling, it was good to see you win that race. Those colored boys are about half the team, they've been doing most of the scoring for the old U. S. A. so far. Less see, Jefferson in the dashes, King in the broad jump, yep, Rufe King in the broad jump, and Crane in the hurdles . . ."

"Jeff was in the relays, Doc, he was in the 400 meter relays, too."

"So he was. Jeff in the 400 meter relays."

"Say, maybe these Germans don't know that. *Der Angriff*, that's one of the big Berlin dailies, comments on it every single day. Yesterday they said our team would be useless without our colored athletes, *Hilksvoelker*, servants, they called 'em."

"No!"

"Right. I saw that, too, and didn't understand it at the time."

" 'Nother thing. They hardly mentioned the Duke's victory."

"I'll say," spoke up a man from Harry's bed.

"Day after his race they had two columns about a fräulein who won the discus throw, and only a short paragraph about the 1,500 meter run. They certainly don't play up the strangers in these parts."

Casey knocked his pipe on the floor. "Believe me, I've been in some queer places and some strange press boxes in my time, but never one like this. The press box, well, usually you think of it as a place for working reporters. Not this one. It's full of girls and boys; who they are I dunno, but their idea seems to be to yell their heads off when any German wins. And can they yell!"

"You bet they can. I seem to notice a change in these people since the Games began."

From his knees, the Duke looked up. "Funny, I was saying that very thing this afternoon. They've put on a marvelous show and won some grand victories and the whole thing seems to have gone to their heads."

"That's right. They yell and holler in your face as if to say: 'Look at us, we won the war' —I beg your pardon, the Games." Casey grinned.

"D'you notice, also, you have to be careful how you use some words round here?" A sports-writer was talking. "They hang their words kinder close to their lips in this man's town. Last night I had dinner in Berlin with some German friends of the family. They never once mentioned Hitler; they called him Herr Schmidt. Right in their own home, too. And they never talked about soldiers, they were always SS men or Storm Troopers or whatever it is they are."

"They may not be soldiers, but I swear I never saw so many uniforms in any one place in my life. Hey, Bill?"

"Me, too."

"Right."

"Well, boys, that about finishes the old packing job." The Duke jammed some dirty underclothes into his suitcase and rose to survey the littered room.

"Say, Duke, you wouldn't care to give us a release on your turning, would you?" The room, ever hopeful, became alert and silent. He shook his head and was about to say something when the door flew open and Slips entered. His face was red, he was breathing fast, he was hot, and he had evidently been hurrying.

"Duke! There you are . . ."

"Hi, Slips, I missed you at dinner. Was just coming over to your place."

But the other paid no attention.

"What's this about your leaving tomorrow for Paris?"

"Why, yes, Slips, I'm sort of tired of it now. My release from the team was all ready and signed a couple of weeks ago, so I'm pushing off. But I'll see you before . . ."

"Look here, boy." He reached out and put a restraining hand on the Duke's arm. "You mustn't leave now." A hush fell upon the room. Every reporter felt he was on the edge of a good story. They looked from the face of the disheveled coach to the tall figure of his protégé. Something was about to break.

"Can't leave for Paris? Says who, Slips?"

"Never mind who. You just can't go, that's all. They've picked you to go to England day after tomorrow to run in the U.S.A.–British Empire Games in London. Team's been made up half an hour ago."

Again that silence. The Duke's voice was disturbed. "But, Slips, honestly I just don't want to go over to London. This English meet wasn't on the program when I left New York, no one mentioned it to me, and now they suddenly want me to run because I won the 1,500 meters. I came over for the Olympics. So there's no obligation on me to compete over in London if I don't feel like it. And I don't."

"No obligation, Duke, but that's not the point. Point is—"

"No, look, Slips, the point is I came over to run in the Olympics in Berlin. Thanks to you I was lucky enough to reach my peak on race day. That's that. Everything else is anticlimax. I'm like everyone round here, I'm sick of running. I couldn't run again so soon to save my life."

"That's all true, but bear in mind what's at stake."

"All I can see is that this meet over in London, like the one in Hamburg and the one in Cologne and all these post-Olympic affairs, is just a gag to attract a crowd and make some money for the A.A.U. Everyone feels the same way I do; we're tired of the Games and running and the whole darn business."

"Duke, I'm afraid . . . well, I'm afraid you'll have to go to London and run just the same."

"Slips, I'm afraid I can't."

16

The engines were still roaring and the passengers were climbing aboard the Air France plane that gloomy morning, yet still he did not show up. They had telephoned Cooks together the night before to reserve the seat next to hers, and he knew it left at nine sharp; but at three minutes before the hour there was no Duke. Overslept? Wrong airport? These possibilities didn't seem likely. No one could mistake the Tempelhof Field. So she resigned herself to his missing the bus and started to climb aboard, when, turning on the upper step, she saw his tall figure rushing through the gateway followed by two porters with his bulging bags. He waved at her, and a minute later dropped into the seat by her side. The door slammed, was locked, a German officer at the side gave a military salute, and the machine began to bump over the ground. It twisted around, the engines roared louder, then, gathering speed, it shot down the runway and into the air over the heart of Berlin. He looked at her expressively, shook his head, took off his hat and wiped his forehead, and shoved his coat in the rack above. Down below was *Unter Den Linden* decked with flags and Olympic banners.

"Things been happening since we saw each other yesterday. D'you hear? If not you must be the only person in the Olympic Village who didn't."

"No? What? What happened?"

"Didn't want me to leave. It seems I was chosen to go to London on the team to run in the U.S.A—British Empire Games next Saturday. Slips came over and told me late last night, practically said I'd have to go. There's an awful mess . . ."

"Oh, Duke. Why didn't you go? You could

have come to France later. It didn't really matter when you came to France, you could have picked us up . . ."

"Wasn't that. Point is I didn't want to go to London to run. Or anywhere else to run, because I'm sick and tired of running and training. This thing must have been more of a strain than I realized; do you know I'm beaten, even today. Couldn't run a hundred yards if I tried. No fooling. It's tough on Slips because he's coach of the team, and of course the Jefferson thing complicates it."

"I heard about Jeff. He's turning professional or something, isn't he?"

"Yes. He's had so many offers from home he's decided to turn pro and his manager—sure, he's got a manager already—won't let him run anywhere on this side, 'cause if he runs and gets beaten folks in the States won't want to see him. He won't be worth anything."

"Why, who could beat Jeff? Isn't he yards faster than anyone else in his event?"

"I know, but that colored boy is like me. I know just how he feels. Now it's over he's sick of running and competition and all that and he's slack. He might lose to some palooka if he went out to run. His manager knows this, so does he. There's too much at stake. Last night they said his offer was $25,000 and he can't afford to take chances. Well, this leaves the A.A.U. holding the bag, understand? Two of their best men and Olympic winners don't show up at London. The worst of it is it makes things awfully bad from my angle."

"But how does Jefferson affect you?"

"Don't you see? Everyone knows pretty well he's turning pro, in fact he's said so. They all want to know if I am, and by not running in London it makes it look as if I was."

"What do you care? You aren't, are you?"

"No. But Slips pointed out last night that if I don't go over it would be, what's he call it, misinterpreted. See, he's on the spot. He got the job as assistant coach because he was a friend of Ernest Brewer, the president of the A.A.U. Now the A.A.U. has this meet scheduled in London, and if we send a good team and if there's a race between Jefferson and that English sprinter, Baker, and one between Brocklehurst and me, there'll be 90,000 there and they'll get a big cut on the gate. Understand? But if Jeff and I don't show up . . ."

"If *you* and Jeff don't show up, you mean. They want you because they all hope to see you race Brocklehurst again."

"All right. But I'm sick and tired of it. I'm still exhausted after the other day. It's too much. I didn't sleep the two nights after that race. Besides, they never picked me until last night. First I hear about it was when Slips came over to the room and told me. We had an argument, and he was hard to refuse, but I don't think I ought to run any more and I won't. You see I went through all this sort of thing last winter at college when the coach there entered me in a big meet in New York without my knowledge, and I had to run although I was sick with the flu. Once is enough."

"If you feel that way about it, fine. Stick to your decision."

"Oh, it's easy enough now, sitting here with you in this plane. But last night with Slips it was tough. He admitted they were wrong, notifying me at the last minute, and that he didn't blame me for not wanting to run. You see Brewer is on his neck to get me, and he's obligated to Brewer. I never really saw Slips upset as he was last night. We had it hot and heavy, while the sportswriters all waited outside in the hall. Great stuff for them, you know. This morning I had a time. Tried to make an early getaway at seven-thirty, but they must have been sleeping in relays on the steps; there they were, a couple of them followed my taxi. Luckily I had a driver that knew English and he took me to the whatd'youcallit, the Friedrichstrasse station, where we circled round and finally lost them in the traffic and then dodged out to Tempelhof. Fast work, wasn't it?"

Was it, though? The plane finally came in sight of the smoky Paris suburbs, over the airdrome of Le Bourget, fluttered down slowly, engines off, slid to earth, bumped along the ground, then turned round and moved up beside the airport. The passengers reached for their coats. The Duke descended with Helen in fine spirits. The disputes of the previous evening were over and done with. He'd made up his mind not to run in London and that was that. Paris, for the first time, and with someone he liked. At one side an enormous two-decked plane marked IMPE-RIAL AIRWAYS was warming up; the mail plane for India, very likely. Beyond a German Luft-hansa was taking off for Berlin. Excitement was in the air. He felt freer and happier than he had for months as he took her arm and went into the customs, when he was brought unpleasantly back to earth.

"Mr. Wellington?"

"Yes."

"Huston, of the A.P." A newspaperman. Just when he'd figured he had thrown them off the track. "The A.A.U. in Berlin has given out your name on the team to run in London, and announced you'll positively meet this man Brocklehurst again. Do you expect to go over?" He was blue-eyed, nice-looking, with a frank glance, and the Duke found it hard to dislike him. But not the six or seven others who suddenly appeared from nowhere and started to bombard him with questions.

"Is it true you won't run next week in the Empire Games?"

"Are you going to turn professional in New York next month?"

"What are your plans if you don't run in London; expect to run anywhere else?"

"Care to say anything about this report from home that you'll turn professional and meet Schumacher in the winter? . . ."

He was bewildered by the barrage of questions. No . . . yes . . . no . . . no . . . no intention to turn pro . . . or run any more . . . or anywhere else . . . no plans for the future. He tried to get away to find his baggage to go through the customs, but they persisted, still at his heels, writing down his monosyllabic utterances on the backs of envelopes, the edges of newspapers, or on yellow paper. He perceived that he hadn't been as smart as he thought in Berlin. "How did you know I was coming in on this plane?" he asked the A.P. man.

"Oh, our Berlin office advised us."

"Oh . . ." No, he wasn't so smart after all. But Helen was. "Quick, I've got a taxi." The reporters, who had already piled into the big blue bus of the Air France Company, immediately piled out in search of another taxi. But this was France. There was no other taxi. Planes had been landing all morning and for the moment no taxi was to be had. The Duke drove out with Helen, leaving the reporters gesticulating with the owner of a private car which they were trying to hire for the pursuit.

A telegram was waiting for Helen at the little hotel on a street bordering the Seine. It was from her family saying the boat had been delayed and they would not arrive in Paris until evening.

"Let's have lunch and go to the Louvre this afternoon." He had only a vague notion of the Louvre as a picture gallery of some sort, but he was glad enough to have his mind taken off the unpleasant situation in which he found himself, for he realized now that one couldn't avoid a problem of this sort simply by moving from one city to another. Once you became a champion you were public property.

After lunch they wandered through the endless halls of the Louvre. At least he wasn't having reporters on his neck. Then turning a corner he saw it enshrined at the end of a long vista: the white "Winged Victory." Exactly like the picture on the wall of the living room at home, yet absolutely different, too. He gazed at the piece of marble as they walked toward it slowly. The closer they came the more beautiful it was.

"Now, I think I understand."

"Understand what?"

"What he said, Keats, wasn't it? 'A thing of beauty is a joy forever.' That never meant a thing to me before. Now I understand." They stood together speechless before the statue. Right then a little black-eyed man came up panting.

"S'cuse me. Mr. Wellington? Thought it was you . . . from your picture. International News Service; been round to the hotel and the concierge said you were over here at the Louvre. Say, we have a despatch from our Berlin office that the A.A.U. assured London this afternoon you'd run against Brocklehurst. Care to comment on it?" In his hand was the back of an envelope. He stood waiting.

17

If there was anything he disliked it was breakfast in his room; but he decided that breakfast
in his room would be more prudent in view of
the battle the previous night when, after meeting
Helen's mother and sister at the Gare St. Lazare,
he was forced to fight his way up to bed through
a barrage of questioning reporters waiting in the
tiny lobby of the hotel. Now he saw that like
every champion he was seized by the great octopus of organized athletics from which he could

struggle but never completely free himself. Through no fault of his own, or anyone's, he was caught. The breakfast arrived and with it the Paris edition of the New York *Herald*. He was thankful that at least the hotel was old fashioned and there was no telephone connection outside in the room. Then a headline on the first page caught his eye.

"BROCKLEHURST-WELLINGTON DUEL OFF?"

"AMERICAN STAR ARRIVES IN PARIS. WON'T RUN IN EMPIRE GAMES. Duke Wellington, the Olympic 1,500 meter champion, arrived by Air France plane from Berlin yesterday declaring that he had no intention of competing in the British Empire—U.S.A. Games at the White City in London next Saturday. Meanwhile Ernest Brewer, the president of the A.A.U., stated definitely over the telephone from Berlin that there was a misunderstanding and that Wellington would run. With 50,000 seats sold already in expectation of a Wellington-Brocklehurst contest on Saturday, and a sellout assured in the Stadium in London, confusion—"

"Yes, come in."

"*Telegramme, M'sieur.*"

He was accustomed to the German telegrams,

and now this French one was still different, very different from a Western Union wire at home. He opened it with difficulty, tearing it clumsily. It was signed Slips. "Will be in Paris on early plane today. Please give no more interviews. Best regards." And dated an hour before. Already he was on his way. No more interviews! Holy smoke, he didn't enjoy the interviews. For the first time he dreaded seeing Slips; he also dreaded the cables which started coming in from New York. What had seemed a simple matter of yes or no, of running or not running, of the wishes of the person most concerned, himself, had, thanks to the press, become a complicated affair and an international sporting incident. He got very warm reading the *Herald* and seeing himself as a world figure, something he didn't like at all, nor did he like what they were saying about him. He wouldn't run, he was turning professional, he wasn't turning professional; sportswriters, columnists, men he'd never seen, all became eloquent on the subject of his life. It wasn't a pleasant thing to read.

But it was the same old Slips, the man he loved, who came to his room straight from the airport. The Duke hadn't gone out and had seen no one except Helen and the various maids and valets who knocked every few minutes with cards or messages from people waiting in the hall below. Not the American newspapermen only; for this was an incident concerning several nations, and British papers as well as the French press sent round their representatives. He was thankful when Slips appeared, thankful, too, at seeing that it was Slips himself, not the nervous and worried man who came to his bungalow that night in the Olympic Village, but the man who had pushed and pulled and helped and encouraged him to the place where he was, 1,500 meter champion. That made it all so difficult. But directly Slips had thrown aside his coat and hat they were intimates once more.

He sat there in that familiar pose, hands on his knees, leaning slightly forward. "Now get this, Duke. I haven't come down to ask any favor of you." Right away he felt better because he knew it would be hard to refuse if Slips asked something for himself.

"Brewer's angry. I'm down here on my own, strictly on my own, paying my fare to see Duke Wellington. Maybe to save you from some trouble, boy. Just remember one thing. No matter what happens we're friends, you and I." He held out that long, firm, muscular hand, and the Duke grabbed it with relief.

"Oh, Slips, I'm so glad you came. Yep, we'll always be friends no matter what happens, don't worry."

"Good. Now order me some lunch. They don't serve food on these darned foreign planes as they do at home. Sit down and don't forget, I'm not going to ask any favor of you or anything for myself." This was the same man who came across the room that afternoon in the fieldhouse in Cambridge just before the Yale meet when he was lying on the mat, frightened and cold, and covered him up with a blanket. The problem, which had seemed so unsolvable, now was simple enough. Slips would fix things up. Slips would arrange it. The lunch came and he attacked it with gusto. Then he lit a cigarette and went over to the window looking down on a line of barges moving slowly up the Seine.

"Now here it is, boy. Brewer's pretty sick about the whole thing. You know he's an awfully good guy, sure he is, I know him, but everyone jumps on him as head of the American Olympics Committee. Some sportswriter said the other day that all the kind things which had been said about Ernest Brewer could be written on a postage stamp, and that's about right. But he's been under terrific pressure for over a year now. First there was raising the money to send the team to Berlin. Did you ever try to raise $250,000? I helped a little this spring, and I found out one thing. When you go to see a banker for money and he stands up, the interview is over." He smiled. The Duke smiled. Same old Slips. This was better. Everything would come out all right.

"Remember, I just want you to see Brewer's point of view. Up to the last night in New York we didn't know whether there would be enough money to get the whole team abroad or not. And it all fell on him; he was the president and responsible. Then came that girl on the boat who got drunk and had to be fired from the squad, and you recall what a beating he took from that. Then Jefferson has been a pain in the neck ever since we landed in Germany. That colored boy is a grand runner but he's a prima donna, and he's had a large pro offer and won't tell anyone whether he's accepted it or not. Then he ups and announces he will not run in the Empire Games in London, which hurts Brewer after we'd promised him to the English authorities. Then on top of all this you walk out. . . ."

"Walk out! But I never walked in, Slips, old boy. That's just the point."

"Sure, I know, I know. But try to see it from Brewer's point of view. The star runners on the team all quitting when it's understood they'll appear in London. . . ."

"Understood by whom? Certainly not by any of us on the team. Why, most of us never knew there were these meets after the Games until they stuck up those notices on the bulletin boards, and even the ones who were picked like me weren't notified until a day or so before leaving. Listen, Slips. If this London thing had been part of the original program, if it had been agreed on before we left New York, it would be up to everyone on the team to run there just as much as in Berlin. But it wasn't. It was something sprung on us at the last moment. How about seeing things from my point of view? I made the team without any help from Brewer, didn't I? The fact is he didn't know I existed until the finish of the 1,500 meters last week. Then he was Duke-ing me like everyone else."

"Boy, you're so hard on people. . . ."

"I'm just trying to explain my point of view. And it's the point of view of everyone on the team. Who won that 1,500 meters? You and I. Yes, you did, you made me, helped me, encouraged me, brought me along; you knew I had the stuff when no one else did, when I didn't; you told me just how to run the race, how to beat Brocklehurst, you told me to forget Lou . . . and I went out and did it. All right. Then without any warning or asking me or anything, when my official release from the team was signed and in my pocket, they go and slap me on that team to go to London. Why? To have another race with Brocklehurst and bring in fifty or sixty thousand bucks to the A.A.U. Say, all the athletes get out of this is a view from a train window; the A.A.U. gets the dough."

"Now look here, Duke. . . ."

"Slips, I'm not a sophomore at Cambridge any more. I've been round. I'm in the middle of things, I'm on the inside now. I came over to run in the Olympics and I gave everything I had in that race. So much I was unconscious afterward, remember? *I* certainly do, I can feel that pain in my eyeballs right now and still see those red spots before my eyes. Took me half an hour almost to pull myself together. Now they suddenly go and put me on this team for some meet in London. . . ."

"The U.S.A.—British Empire Games aren't just 'some meet.' They're a regular fixture, they've been held after every Olympics since 1924."

"I don't care. I wanted to make the Olympic team for two reasons. The main one was because I wanted to run. But I also knew if I did well it would help me get a coaching job in some school next year. Running in the Olympics is one thing. Running in exhibitions is something else. I'm sick of running. I'm bushed now. If Brocklehurst can, and wants to, that's his affair. I can't. And I don't care whether we beat the English or not, what's more." His face was flushed and he was determined, and Slips saw his task was difficult. This boy wasn't just another college boy. College . . . His mind left the room and the red plush daycouch and the blue sky of France outside, and moved back to another familiar scene in Dunster H 35 in Cambridge. There was Thurber the president of the Circle and the captain of the track team trying to persuade this green sophomore to come out and run; there was Whitney, the distance man and veteran miler, tall, sinewy and quiet; and there was Mickey Mcguire, the Duke's roommate, sitting back with a twinkle in his eye enjoying the whole scene. The Duke was talking. "It's a funny place, Harvard, but it does give you a sense of values. What for do I want to waste my time plugging round the track when I can get something much better . . ."

And Thurber's Bostonian accent breaking in.

"But your exercise, man, you've got to exercise."

"Exercise! Thurber, that's the old gag I first heard freshman year. Used to fall for it then. I went down and gave everything I had for football, and at night I was so tired I couldn't study. Good for nothing. The result—probation and one year of hell." Say what you liked about Harvard, it was a tough place, but it managed to turn out individuals. He came back again to the little room with its red plush furniture, everything different except the flushed and determined face of the boy.

". . . mind you, if it's for Slips Ellis, well, sure, anything. If you said it meant a job or something important to you, I suppose I'd come. Otherwise, no, thanks very much."

"I haven't said that, have I?" He was thinking

how this boy had grown up, how he had changed and yet how little he had changed. "Duke, just ask you to remember one thing. The A.A.U. brought you over here, and you owe . . ."

"Hey! Wait a minute. The A.A.U. did *not* bring me over here. The A.A.U. didn't pay five cents of my boat ride. Americans paid it, a million people across the country who made up the kitty, who paid a tax on admission at track meets, who contributed money to the Olympic Fund. The A.A.U. didn't pay my way over, and as for owing them anything, I ran and won, didn't I? That's more than most of the team did. They owe me something, to let me alone. If it hadn't been for them I wouldn't be in this mess right now."

Slips saw he was getting nowhere fast. He had one card left. "I told you I didn't come down here to ask a favor of you, didn't I?" His tone changed, his voice dropped.

"Yes, you did." What was coming?

"You see, Duke, it isn't as simple as you think. Your wishes, I mean. You've been advertised, and everyone in England naturally wants to see whether you'd beat Brocklehurst the second time. You know how we'd feel at home."

"Why did they advertise me without finding out whether I'd run or not?"

"But the stars always compete in these meets."
That was true, too. "So we assumed . . ."

"They'd better hadn't, that's all." Now the
Duke was in earnest. "Slips, it's their funeral.
Maybe I'd feel differently if all this hadn't hap-
pened to me once before, with that son of a gun
Coffman in the Studebaker Mile last winter in
New York."

"Boy, see here. I told you something, I said
I hadn't come down here to ask favors." Well,
here goes. Last chance. "I didn't. It's your old
friend, Slips Ellis talking. I'm asking you to run
over there in London on Saturday as a favor to
an old pal of mine, Duke Wellington."

"What do you mean?" Somehow he felt uneasy
with Slips leaning forward and putting one hand
on his knee. This was serious.

"You spoke about my job. Yes, I guess it
would sort of help things if you ran over at the
Games in London. But that's not very important.
It's not my job, it's *your* job I'm thinking most
about."

"My job? I don't get you, Slips."

"You want to teach in some school and be a
track coach, don't you? All right. If you're serious about that I advise you to run. Because if
you don't, they'll disqualify you, and what school

is going to hire a man as coach who has been disqualified by the A.A.U.? Make up your mind, Duke. It's your future that's at stake. Coaching is a hard-boiled game, and if you quit now your chances of ever getting a job are pretty slim."

"You mean to say . . . that guy Brewer . . ."

"Wait a minute. Don't get Ernest Brewer wrong. He's a good guy, but he has to take the rap for those mugs on the committee. He wouldn't disqualify you, he's angry at you now, but he'll certainly fight your battle in the committee meeting. Just the same, those babies feel they've been responsible for getting you over to Europe, and if you don't race Brocklehurst in London they'll call the committee together and disqualify you. Once barred from competition by the A.A.U.—well, I don't suppose I need explain the effect that would have on a possible coaching job, do I?"

No more explanations were necessary. His getting a job had become important; all important since he had met and known Helen in Berlin. It was more than just a job, it was his right to work, his future, his life with her that was at stake. All this became suddenly and unpleasantly clear. He saw, too, the tentacles of organized sport slowly closing in around him. So that was it! Slips was shooting straight. Brewer, he knew, would never permit such a thing if he could help it. But the vindictive members of the committee, seeing their London gate cut in half, wouldn't hesitate.

"So I'm an amateur athlete, am I? What is an amateur athlete, anyway?" His bitter tone was interrupted as the door opened and the jovial red face of Jim Casey appeared. Trust Casey to get in where no one else could.

"An amateur athlete? Certainly, I'll tell you, boys. An amateur athlete is a boob who has paid for his registration card and doesn't speak disrespectfully of the A.A.U."

18

They leaned together over the wide stone parapet watching the river silvered in the moonlight. Below and to their left, strange blue reflections from the Gare d'Orsay cast a queer glow on the water, and up and down the banks were the sparkle of lights from barges anchored to the shore. An enchanting scene if only that decision wasn't facing him.

"At first, before I knew you well, I wanted Brocklehurst to win that race awfully." She hesitated as she spoke.

He was surprised. "Did you really? Why?"

"Wonder whether you'd get my feelings? It's hard to explain it to myself now because I know you and suffered when you were going through all that on the track below. But I did want Brocklehurst to win at first. There was something so fresh and unspoiled in his whole approach to sport and the Games. If he won, he won; if he didn't, well, all right. His training, for instance. It was different from the regimented German way, and from ours, too. Why, he shocked all our coaches except Slips. The funny thing was they couldn't make anything out of it because he was so good. He smoked a pipe and drank beer and ate about what he liked, and lived such a normal life it was abnormal. I heard old Pop Sanderson sounding off about him one day, but there wasn't much he could say when Brocklehurst had just won his heat in the fastest time of all."

"Yes, Slips told me about that. It gave him a great laugh."

"Slips was there. But I liked the way Brocklehurst ran and I thought it would sort of jar all the coaches and pontiffs on our team if he won. Then I noticed he got such pleasure from his practice, and there was a sense of freedom and liberty in the way he prepared for the race that was refreshing. Certainly one didn't see too much of that spirit up there in Berlin."

"Right. The English still seemed to take it all as a game. They didn't win much, though, did they?"

"That's it. In a way the English in Berlin were the only real amateurs. You know, real amateurs, college and club runners, men who were students or else who worked for a living, not like . . ."

"Like Von Gerhardt. I must say that baby sort of rocked me when he explained how he was part of the state, how he'd been living off the government for three years just so he could win in the Olympics."

"That's it. The English were the only amateurs, not state amateurs or semi-pros, but men who ran because they loved it. And their officials were men who loved sport—not money grabbers or, like the Germans and Italians, regular employees of the state. What did they call that man, the head sports fellow in Berlin. *Reichssportkommissar*. That's it, leader of sport in the Reich. The Olympic Games! Come to think of it, Sparta was the original Fascist state, wasn't it?"

"Say! Never thought of that. Yes, that was the

thing Berlin proved for me. A grand show, selling Germany to the world. But sport, nix. As for the Games, toward the end I felt they were just a pretext, and that's one reason I was so unhappy and so glad to get away with you."

"Certainly was a great demonstration and a marvelous pageant staged by a great regime, not a meeting of girls who loved to fence and boys who loved to run and jump. Seems to me the Games weren't an end but a means. Today we don't serve the ideals of sport any more, we serve ourselves from it. Take Von Gerhardt, take Schumacher, take Jefferson, take . . ."

"Take Wellington."

"No such thing. No, Duke, you won't go that way."

"If I run over there in London I do. And if I don't how'm I ever going to get a job. And a job's mighty important right now. Six weeks ago, Helen, I hadn't the vaguest idea what I'd do after leaving college. For one thing I didn't want to quit running, suddenly, like that; I hated to stop all at once just because I'd left college the way most men do; it seemed terrible to give up something you loved just because you weren't running for your school any more. And I hated to get slowed up and heavy, the way most of the older graduates that came back to Cambridge were. Then came the trip to Berlin and Slips on the boat, and I realized what I wanted to do was what he's done, be a coach, a decent coach, a darn good track coach, which would mean I could stay with it and keep on running as long as I liked for myself. All right. Then I met you. Now, well, now of course it's the job that's vital. It makes my decision to run or not run over in London so much more important than if just only my future was held up. If I don't do what those babies say, how shall I ever land a job, Helen? Did I tell you Slips brought me a letter from Ernest Brewer this afternoon when he came down. Nice letter. Oh, yes, awfully nice, full of fatherly advice but sort of putting it up to me. He explained—you know, I'm-older-than-you-are stuff—one gets more out of life by compromising occasionally than by being stubborn. . . ."

She gave a gesture of impatience. "Compromise! That's what brought the Olympic Games to the place they're in now, that's what has put sport where it is. Never mind people who talk to you of expediency and compromise. That's a coward's way. I should think you could do better than that. See, here's where you must make a decision. . . ."

"Decisions! I'm always forced to make decisions. Why is it? When I came to Cambridge freshman year I got on probation at the November Hours and had to decide whether to stay and study or go home for Christmas. Was I homesick! Then the decision to run. You see I'd promised Father to make the Dean's List and they found out I could run and wanted me to come out for track. So they came round and hinted they'd make me a member of the Circle, the big sophomore club if I'd come out. Did I? Sure, but I didn't join the Circle. Another decision. Why don't other people have decisions to make?"

"They do, stupid. Everyone does. We all have decisions. That's life; decisions. See here, when you were in college they brought pressure on you to run."

"I'll say they did. Kept coming up to my room after me the whole time."

"Did you run?"

"Yes, I ran. But not for their reasons. It would have been much easier not to have run, to have done nothing."

"Yes, and it would have been easier to

have gone home for your Christmas vacation, wouldn't it?"

"You bet! I'll never forget that Christmas alone. My first Christmas away from home, too."

"Well, if you've never taken the easiest way out, why on earth begin now?"

"Don't you understand? I love running, I love to run. Not now maybe, not after that agony up in Berlin, not in the middle of this mess; but in a few months, when it's all over, when I'm forgotten and out of the sports pages, then the urge to run will return. I know it will because it's a part of me. Suppose that's really what pulled me out on the track on Soldier's Field, the yen to run, the desire for the feel of cinders under my feet, the spring smell as we jogged up the river-bank, and the sun, and the warmth, and friends running beside me, all of that, not just because I disliked those Circle men. I didn't honestly care about them. But something stronger, something inside me, you know."

"If you think I don't, you're crazy. That's the way I feel about fencing. The game, the sport, not only winning. Olympic 1,500 meter champion, Duke Wellington of Iowa. All right, tell me the name of the man who won the 1,500 meters in the 1928 Games. Or last time, even."

"That's it. You get me. Through Slips Ellis and running I grew up at Cambridge. Gosh, that was a long while ago. You can't help feeling for something which has been a part of you over a period of years, can you, Helen? Of course not. Sure, I'd love to run in the woods, anywhere. But how can you do that if you work in a city office? That's why I wanted to teach, to coach, to stay with it, not suddenly be cut off from all running merely because some old men on a committee in a room in Berlin feel they aren't getting enough of a gate from this extra meet in London. Then on top of it all comes the question of a job, of work, of earning a living. . . ."

"Hold on. You've been up against this before. Oh, I know, not as vital perhaps, but it must have seemed pretty vital at the time. Well, you've always taken a chance and stuck your neck out for what you felt, haven't you? And you've come out all right, haven't you?"

"Yes, but this is different. A job today . . ."

"I don't care what's at stake; it really isn't different at all except that it happens to be more important. If you'd played safe all your life you wouldn't be Duke Wellington and you wouldn't be here and anyway I wouldn't like you. There's only one thing for you to do."

"Right. Only one thing to do. I never quit before, why should I give in now?"

"Good boy. And don't worry, you'll land something, I know you will; you'll come out on top. . . ."

"Yes, but, Helen, how'll I ever explain things to those newspaper boys? You'll understand, so will Slips, but they won't. And watch them misrepresent my point of view, a lot of birds who never ran, who only know sport from what they see in the grandstand, who talk about 'thrills,' who'll suggest I'm afraid to take a chance running Brocklehurst again, that the Berlin race was a fluke. How can I escape them, where can I go. . . ."

"Wait a second. Here's an idea. What night is it?"

"Monday. No, Tuesday."

"Great! Tomorrow's Wednesday. All right, you've decided. You've made up your mind. Here's where I can help."

19

The sign over the track in the long trainshed read: "C. G. T. TRAIN POUR LE NORMANDIE. NORMANDIE BOAT TRAIN. 9:48."

He stood by the gate, waiting. Passengers rushed up with that queer fixed look on their faces that people have when going to the boat train. Behind each traveler was a porter in a blue striped uniform buried under bags, suitcases, hat boxes, especially hat boxes. The Duke had never seen so many hat boxes in one place before in his life.

At last she came—just when it was danger-
ously near train time and he was wondering
whether the plan had fallen through. Her face
was aglow as she weaved through the crowd and
saw him standing beside the gate. Back of her
was a porter with his bags hung through a strap
over his shoulder, and the Duke was glad he
had failed to take advantage of the generous
distribution of Olympic Team stickers that might
have been plastered over his baggage and given
the show away. He was happy to see her, for
her plan that he spend the night alone in a strange
hotel across the river from their own was not
pleasant. He had slept little. But even through
his relief at seeing her, at knowing that his decision was all made and knowing, also, that it
was the right one, he felt a pang. He was leaving
this girl who'd been with him through the most
difficult days of his life.

"All right?"

"Yes, but not easy. We packed everything
last night and had the bags down at the baggage
entrance where they wouldn't be seen, but when
we finished there was no one up to whom we
could pay the bill. I was so afraid they'd find
out your bill was being paid this morning. Then
when I came down they watched me, thinking

you were upstairs in your room, but being aw-fully suspicious just the same. So I let them watch me drive away in a taxi, had him go round the block and park below the hotel, and then he went in and brought your bags from the baggage room."

"Wonderful. Only let's not cheer too soon. Remember Berlin where I thought I'd pulled a fast one?"

"Do I? Seen anyone?"

"Oh, there's no one here."

"Got your ticket?"

"No, I must get that aboard the boat. I've bought a ticket to Havre and a platform ticket for you to come through the gate with me. C'm'on." They passed through onto the platform crowded with milling passengers all in their best traveling clothes, furs and flowers, and the general air of being about to set out on a transatlantic voyage. "Let's go to my car. There might be reporters here who would recognize me from my pictures. Car Z, seat 4, compartment 2. It's second class. I ought to be safe enough there. When they asked me I gave your name."

She caught his arm. "You didn't! Oh, I'm sure you're all right now."

A voice from a loudspeaker rang over the platform. *"En voiture, en voiture, s'il vous plaît, mes-sieurs-dames."* The groups began to dissolve and mount the train, as they threaded their way down toward Car Z, which was in the front. The porter climbed aboard, found the place in a crowded compartment, and put up his bags, while the Duke followed and gave him some change. Then he went after the porter who was working his way past the gazers at the windows of the corridor to the entrance of the car.

"All set? Good-bye, Duke. I'm glad you've decided, but I guess I'm sorry you have to leave."

"Good-bye, Helen." In spite of the reporters and the general mess on this side of the Atlantic, he suddenly found he didn't want much to leave. He wanted to stay. But most of all he wanted to kiss her. He leaned down and kissed her just as the train gave a creak and moved slowly. She turned and, jumping to the step, swung herself to the ground.

"Take care of yourself. . . ."

"See you in New York. . . ." He felt silly, as a conductor pushed rudely before him in an attempt to shut the outside door. On the platform, moving along with the train, he saw Helen with a smile on her face, and he also saw three perspiring and excited men with hats on the backs of their heads. One of them noticed him in the vestibule and jumped on the step of the car, evidently prepared to get a story if it was necessary to ride to Le Havre. Too late. The conductor was uninterested in American reporters and their troubles. He banged the door in his face as the train gathered momentum, and although the two companions ran beside the car, gesticulating and shouting questions, the Duke could hear nothing. He was safe.

"ST. LAZARE 550 M." said a big red sign painted on the white stone of the cut through which they were moving. The Iron Duke, winner of the 1,500 meter Olympic run, was going home.

He went mechanically back into the compartment and cleared his seat. The carriage was full, everyone fussing with bundles and arranging bags in the racks. The train went faster and entered the suburbs of the city. There was a small station named ASNIERES. He wondered how it was pronounced. His seven fellow passengers, all Americans, lapsed into a general complaint about the French who, it appeared, did things in such strange ways. They didn't serve butter with dinner or ice water with meals, they always expected to be tipped and never delivered goods when they promised them.

He listened without really hearing them, his spirits low because the thing that had been hanging over him was settled at last and the tension was over. He was also low because now he was alone. Helen would not be there for lunch and dinner. The Duke was alone, going home to his family, to Waterloo, Iowa, to lots of people who wouldn't understand his point of view and why he didn't want to run. It was all very difficult. The worst of it was that he was leaving Helen and returning without a job or any chance of one. The newspaper in his lap slipped to the floor and, as he leaned over, a headline with his name stared up at him.

BROCKLEHURST-WELLINGTON DUEL OFF
ENGLISHMAN OVERTRAINED: WONT RUN

For a few seconds things spun round, everything was blurred; he couldn't see, couldn't think. But with Brocklehurst out, it wouldn't matter whether he ran or not. Was it really true, was it actually so?

"London. Tuesday. Cecil G. V. Brocklehurst,

the English distance star who ran the sensational 1,500 meters with Duke Wellington in the Olympic Games in Berlin last week, has decided not to compete in the British Empire vs. U. S. A. Games in the White City Stadium in London on Saturday. Brocklehurst states that he is overtrained and will do no more running this season."

It *was* true. Brocklehurst wouldn't run. And if he didn't, their duel was off and no one would care whether the Duke competed in London or not. Because there wouldn't be anyone for him to run against, and no reason, therefore, why he shouldn't stay out of the meet, too. It was over! The whole trouble, this horrible mess which had been such a nightmare since the night Slips Ellis rushed into his room in Berlin, was over and settled. Then all at once it struck him. Gosh. He needn't go home!

Through the car window the sun was shining and the train was passing a small suburban station with pink geraniums planted in borders beside the track and small white houses with red tiled roofs in the little town beyond. He didn't have to go home. He didn't have to go home now. It was possible—yes, he could take the first train back from Le Havre, and have that trip through France with Helen. Now he realized that the worst thing about going wasn't the decision and all it meant but leaving Helen behind. Now he didn't have to leave her.

Still a little dizzy from the shock he tried to collect himself, to think. Then he understood. Of course! That was what the reporters at the station were trying to tell him: that Brocklehurst wasn't going to run. Well, anyway, he'd read the paper and found it out before he bought his ticket on the boat. Imagine getting on board and out of sight of land and finally discovering the whole thing had been settled by the Englishman's withdrawal. For it had been settled. To make sure he wasn't wrong he reread the whole paragraph. No, there it was in black and white: Brocklehurst wouldn't run. And probably there were lots of fools who'd say he wasn't running because he was afraid of the Duke. Apparently Brocklehurst had had a decision to make, too.

Other books in the Odyssey series:

William O. Steele
- ☐ THE BUFFALO KNIFE
- ☐ FLAMING ARROWS
- ☐ THE PERILOUS ROAD
- ☐ WINTER DANGER

Edward Eager
- ☐ HALF MAGIC
- ☐ KNIGHT'S CASTLE
- ☐ MAGIC BY THE LAKE
- ☐ MAGIC OR NOT?
- ☐ SEVEN-DAY MAGIC
- ☐ THE TIME GARDEN
- ☐ THE WELL-WISHERS

Anne Holm
- ☐ NORTH TO FREEDOM

John R. Tunis
- ☐ IRON DUKE
- ☐ THE DUKE DECIDES
- ☐ CHAMPION'S CHOICE
- ☐ THE KID FROM TOMKINSVILLE
- ☐ WORLD SERIES
- ☐ KEYSTONE KIDS
- ☐ ROOKIE OF THE YEAR
- ☐ ALL-AMERICAN
- ☐ YEA! WILDCATS!
- ☐ A CITY FOR LINCOLN

Henry Winterfeld
- ☐ DETECTIVES IN TOGAS
- ☐ MYSTERY OF THE ROMAN RANSOM

Look for these titles and others in the Odyssey series in your local bookstore.

Or send payment in the form of a check or money order to: HBJ (Operator J), 465 S. Lincoln Drive, Troy, Missouri 63379.

Or call: 1-800-543-1918 (ask for Operator J).

☐ I've enclosed my check payable to Harcourt Brace Jovanovich.

Charge my: ☐ Visa ☐ MasterCard ☐ American Express.

Card Expiration Date

Card #

Signature

Name

Address

City   State   Zip

Please send me _____ copy/copies @ $3.95 each.

($3.95 x no. of copies) $ _____

Subtotal $ _____

Your state sales tax   + $ _____

Shipping and handling   + $ _____
($1.50 x no. of copies)

Total $ _____

PRICES SUBJECT TO CHANGE